P9-CMR-423

PEGGY MORELAND
THE RESTLESS VIRGIN

SILHOUETTE *Desire*®

Published by Silhouette Books

America's Publisher of Contemporary Romance

SILHOUETTE BOOKS

ISBN 0-373-76163-5

THE RESTLESS VIRGIN

Printed in U.S.A.

Prologue

Double-Cross Heart Ranch
1988

Sam backed her horse trailer up to the dark barn, using her brake lights for illumination, then climbed wearily from the cab of her truck. Groaning, she pressed her hands to her lower back and stretched out the kinks placed there by the seven-hour drive from Oklahoma. With nothing but her horse and a radio for company, the trip had been long and lonely.

But Sam was used to going it alone. When her driver's license had arrived in the mail shortly after her sixteenth birthday, designating her a legal driver, her father had handed her the keys to a truck along with the news bulletin that he wouldn't be hauling her butt—or her horse's either for that matter—across the country anymore. If she wanted to try for a national barrel-racing title, he'd told her, she'd be doing it alone. He didn't have the time.

No surprise there. Lucas McCloud rarely had time for his daughters.

But tonight, Sam thought wistfully, she could have used a little company on the long trip home. She had hoped that Mandy, her older sister, would make the trip to Oklahoma with her, but with the baby and all, Mandy no longer had the freedom to take off at a moment's notice. And Merideth... Sam snorted at the idea of her younger sister tagging along. Merideth wouldn't be caught dead at a rodeo. The thought of rubbing shoulders with cowboys, getting dust on her shoes, or possibly even breaking a nail was too horrifying for her.

Sam sighed and scuffed her way wearily to the rear of the truck where she unhooked the back doors and lowered the ramp. "Come on, Skeeter," she called gently to the tall roan. "We're home." Slipping her fingers beneath his halter, she clipped the lead rope into place, then guided him down to solid ground.

Rather than turn on the barn's overhead lights and disturb the other animals, Sam led her horse down the dark alley, relying on memory and moonlight to guide her way. At Skeeter's stall, she opened the door, then braced a hip against it as she shifted to unhook his halter. With a loving pat on his rump, she urged him inside. "'Night, Skeeter," she whispered. "See you in the morning."

Just as she dropped the latch, locking the gate into place, a man stepped from the shadows in the next stall. A scream rose in Sam's throat, but dissolved into a frustrated hiss of air when she recognized the man as Reed Wester, one of her father's ranch hands. She pressed a hand over her thudding heart. "Reed, you nearly scared me to death," she accused him.

He chuckled. "A little jumpy tonight, aren't you, Sam?"

She heaved a breath, trying to slow her heart's racing.

She didn't like Reed. He had a way of looking at her that made her skin crawl. "No, you just startled me." She started to move around him, anxious to get to the house and away from him, but Reed stepped in front of her, blocking her path. Sam snapped up her head to frown at him.

"How'd you do in Guthrie?"

"I ran slack, so I won't know the results until tomorrow, but I held the fastest time when I left." Wearily, she pushed a stray wisp of hair away from her eyes. "If you'll excuse me, I'm tired."

"I'll bet you're a little stiff, too, considerin' that long drive and all." He stepped closer, putting a hand on her arm and running it from elbow to wrist. Goose bumps pebbled Sam's skin while the nauseating smell of cheap whiskey and sweat swirled beneath her nose. "I could give you a rubdown," he offered. "Ease the ache a little. What do ya say?"

Sam jerked free of his grasp, her nostrils pinched in anger. "No thanks," she muttered, brushing past him.

A hand at her arm stopped her, and before she could react, Reed had spun her around and slammed her up against the barn wall, his hands cuffed around her wrists above her head.

"What's the matter, Sam?" he sneered. "You think because you're a McCloud you're too good for the likes of me?"

Terror squeezed Sam's chest at the hatred in his eyes and she tried to press her head farther back against the wall. "N-no," she stammered, fighting hard to hide her fear. "I'm just tired, is all."

He took a step nearer, pressing his body against hers, pinning her harder against the wall. "You won't be for long," he promised, his voice low and menacing. "Reed Wester knows how to make a woman forget most anything."

"Let me go, Reed," she pleaded as she squirmed, trying to break free.

"Ah, come on, Sammie girl. You know you want it. You've been twitchin' that sassy little butt of yours in my face for months, just beggin' for it."

"No!" she cried, horrified that he'd think such a thing. "I haven't. I swear. Just let me go, Reed, please."

He buried his nose at her neck, his breath hot and rancid against her bare skin. "I've watched you ride that horse of yours bareback, watched you squeeze your thighs against his sides. The whole time I imagined it was me those thighs were wrapped around, and me you were pressing that hot crotch against." His teeth grazed her skin. "And I know you were wishin' the same damn thing."

Before Sam could deny his claim, he moved his mouth up her throat, the hard stubble on his jaw scraping against her sensitive skin. The stench of whiskey and sweat grew stronger, making her head swim, her stomach churn. She swallowed back the bile that rose in her throat and forced herself to think. She knew she had to get away from him. But how? All the men who worked the Double-Cross would be asleep in the bunkhouse at this hour, but if she screamed loud enough...

"Let me go, Reed," she warned as she continued to fight his grip on her hands. "Or I swear I'll scream and have every wrangler on the Double-Cross swarming in here."

He quickly shifted her wrists to one meaty hand, then clapped the other over her mouth. "Don't even think about it," he threatened in a low voice. He dropped his hand and Sam quickly sucked in air to scream, but before she could release it, his mouth slammed against hers.

Tears burned behind Sam's closed lids while fear turned every muscle in her body to steel. She wouldn't succumb to him, she told herself. She'd die first. Using every ounce of strength she possessed, she thrust herself hard against him, hoping to unbalance him, then lifted a boot, slamming it down hard on his instep.

He yelped in pain, but didn't loosen his hold on her. "You bitch!" he snarled, ramming his body harder against hers to prevent her from trying the same tactic again. But Sam wasn't through fighting yet. When he dipped his face toward her again, she sank her teeth into his cheek. With a howl, Reed reared back, staring at her in surprise. Then his eyes narrowed dangerously. He closed a hand over her breast and squeezed hard, smiling as her face contorted in pain.

"You shoulda told me you like it rough," he growled, then stabbed his tongue between her parted lips and dug his fingers deeper into her breast.

Sam twisted her head back and forth against the rough barn wall, frantically trying to escape the suffocating pressure of his mouth, the pain his fingers inflicted on her tender flesh. But she was helpless against his greater strength.

A sob rose in her throat. *Please, God, please don't let him do this to me,* she cried silently.

The prayer had barely formed when he tore his mouth from hers. He stared at her, his eyes wild and dark, while a demonic smile twisted his lips. "I been waitin' for this for a long time." He placed a thick finger at the opening of her western blouse, then curled it until it lay in the valley between her breasts. Sam's blood ran cold at the invasion, at the heat and roughness of his calloused finger on her bare flesh.

Chuckling, he muttered, "Let's see what you've got," then jerked the finger down. Buttons rained on the hard-packed dirt floor while Sam shrank against the wall, trying her best to melt into it.

Knowing that this might well be her last and only hope for rescue, she opened her mouth and let loose a scream that she prayed would reach the bunkhouse. Reed slapped a hand over her mouth, knocking her head hard against the wall, then yanked her away from it, twisting her arm behind her back. She managed to suck in one shocked breath before his hand closed over her mouth again.

"You're gonna regret that," he warned her. He shoved her kicking and fighting ahead of him into an empty stall and knocked her down on the scattered straw.

Instinctively, Sam rolled, but before she could escape, he pinned her to the stall floor. Her breath burned in her lungs as she bucked and kicked, trying to escape.

He quickly moved to straddle her. Fumbling for his belt buckle with his free hand, he ordered roughly, "Spread your legs." When she didn't respond, he closed a hand around her throat and squeezed. "I said spread 'em!"

Choking for air, Sam clawed at his fingers.

"What's going on here!"

Reed twisted at the sound of the male voice, giving Sam a view of the open stall door. Gabe Peters, her father's ranch foreman, stood in the opening, aiming a flashlight at the two of them.

Reed tightened his fingers on her neck. "Me and Sam was just havin' us a little fun. Weren't we, Sammie girl?" he prodded, daring her to disagree with him.

"No!" The single word scraped like a dull razor at her closed, raw throat. "Gabe, please," she begged hoarsely while she continued to fight Reed's hold on her, "help me!"

With a feral growl, Gabe tossed the flashlight aside and grabbed Reed by the back of the collar and hauled him to his feet. Footsteps pounded in the alleyway as more wranglers appeared on the scene. Turning, Gabe thrust Reed at the first man who appeared at the stall door. "See that he packs his gear. Then I want you to personally escort him off the Double-Cross." Without questioning the order, four men quickly surrounded Reed and dragged him away.

"And if your fists happen to connect with his face in the process," Gabe yelled after them, "so much the better."

Once the men were out of sight, Gabe dropped to a knee beside Sam, his voice growing gentle. "Honey, are you okay?"

Sam shrank away from his touch, clutching her torn blouse in white-knuckled hands. "I want to go home, Gabe," she said, finally giving in to the tears. "I—I just want to go h-home."

"Just give me a minute to call your daddy and let him know we're—"

She grabbed at his hand, her eyes wild. "No! Please, Gabe. Don't tell Daddy!"

The fact that she didn't want her father to know about the attack didn't surprise Gabe. Lucas McCloud wasn't a man long on comfort. He shrugged out of his denim jacket. "Okay. Okay," he said soothingly. "Settle down now. I'll see you home safe." He draped the jacket across Sam's shoulders. As he started to rise, pulling her up along with him, the overhead lights popped on, their glare blinding after the moonlit darkness of a moment before.

"What the hell is going on in here?"

At the sound of Lucas's angry voice, Gabe turned to look at Sam. The absolute terror in her eyes had him tightening his hold on her. Lucas's temper was legendary, and the fact that his daughters caught the brunt end of it more often than not was common knowledge among the ranch hands. "It's me. Gabe. And Sam," he added, knowing there was no escape for her now.

There was a muffled curse, followed by the sound of determined footsteps, then Lucas appeared in the opening of the stall. Sam clutched tighter at the jacket and Gabe quickly stepped in front of her, offering her more concealment.

"What the hell is going on?" Lucas demanded again.

Heaving a sigh, Gabe explained. "I caught Reed in the

barn with Sam and he was—'' He paused, searching for a gentler way, for Sam's benefit, to explain the incident. ''Well, he was giving her a hard time. But everything's under control now,'' he assured Lucas. ''The boys have taken Reed back to the bunkhouse to pack his gear, then they're going to escort him off the Double-Cross.''

Lucas's face reddened, veins throbbing to life at his temples and on his neck. His entire body trembled with barely suppressed rage as he tightened his hands into fists at his sides. ''Who the hell gave you the authority to fire one of my wranglers? Reed Wester is the best damn horse trainer in the state, and you damn well know it.''

Gabe had always known Lucas's heart was made of stone, but the idea of him coming to the defense of a lowlife like Reed Wester when his own daughter had almost been raped by the man galled Gabe to no end. ''He came dang close to rapin' her, Lucas. If I hadn't heard her scream, I don't—''

Lucas snapped his gaze to Sam, his look scathing. His face turned an even darker shade of red. ''So, you're the cause of all this. I should've known.'' He took a threatening step closer. ''What did you do to provoke him?''

Sam hadn't thought anything could hurt as much as the punishment she'd received at Reed's hands. Her father's words proved her wrong. But she'd be damned if she'd let him see how much he'd hurt her. ''Nothing,'' she replied, lifting her chin. ''Absolutely nothing.''

Lucas narrowed his eyes, sucking in air through his teeth. His mouth curled into a snarl of disgust while a muscle on his jaw flexed. ''Get to the house,'' he ordered.

''Now, Lucas—'' Gabe began, ready to defend Sam.

Lucas wheeled on him. ''Don't you 'now, Lucas' me! It'll be your head that rolls if we lose Reed over this.''

Gabe's back stiffened at the threat, but the rising color on his boss's face made him momentarily set aside his own anger. Ever since Lucas's oldest daughter Mandy had announced that she was carrying Jesse Barrister's baby, his boss's temper—erratic at best—had taken on the volatility of a Texas twister, mowing down anything or anyone who happened to be in his path. And since Mandy's return to the ranch with the baby, things had only gotten worse. Gabe himself had persuaded Lucas to see a doctor, but the stubborn old rancher ignored the doctor's advice, refusing to change his diet or take the medication prescribed. "You need to calm down, Lucas," Gabe warned. "Gettin' upset like this ain't gonna help your blood pressure none."

Sweat glistened on Lucas's face as he lifted a fist and shook it. "To hell with my blood pressure! I've got to find Reed and see if I can salvage this mess y'all've made. Where is he?"

"I told you," Gabe replied patiently. "The boys took him to the bunkhouse and—"

Before Gabe could repeat his explanation, Lucas swayed, grabbing for the stall gate with one hand while clutching at his chest with the other. Gabe made a move to help, but Lucas waved him away. "Leave me be," he growled, his breath coming in short, sharp gasps. Sweat poured down his face and he dipped his head into the crook of the arm braced against the stall door. As he tried to straighten, his knees buckled beneath him. Gabe lunged forward, but before he could reach him, Lucas crumpled to the floor, his fingers sliding down the gate's metal rails, each hit a loud pinging thump in the silent barn.

"Daddy!" Sam screamed, running to drop down beside her father.

Gabe nudged Sam aside, flattening his hand over Lucas's chest, feeling for a heartbeat. When he didn't find one, he turned to her, his expression grave. "Call for an ambulance. I'll stay here and work on him."

Slowly, Sam pushed herself to her feet, her eyes riveted on her father's slack face. As she ran for the phone in the lab room, the memory of her father's words chased her.

So, you're the cause of all this. I should have known. What did you do to provoke him?

Those would be the last words that Lucas McCloud would ever say to his daughter...yet the guilt heaped on Sam's slender shoulders that night would last a lifetime.

One

Austin, Texas
1998

Sam frowned at the scribbled directions she held, trying her darndest to decipher her nephew's scrawled handwriting. When she got back to the Double-Cross, she promised herself, she was going to make arrangements to have a separate phone line installed for her veterinary practice and invest in a good answering machine. And this time she meant it! Unraveling the messages taken by whoever happened to pick up the phone at the main house on the Double-Cross Heart Ranch was a royal pain in the butt.

She glanced up, peering through her truck's bug-splattered windshield at empty pastures thick with overgrown weeds and cedar saplings. Snapped barbed wire coiled crazily along the fence line like a home perm gone bad, while sparrows splashed in a rusted water trough.

Above the crumbling limestone pillars flanking the gate, a faded sign swung.

"Rivers Ranch," she said aloud. Since the name matched that on the message her nephew Jaime had taken, she figured she must have the right place.

And if this is how Nash Rivers takes care of what's his, she added mentally, *it's no wonder he's got a sick horse.*

But his abilities as a rancher weren't her concern, Sam reminded herself. Only his livestock were. Still, having been raised on a ranch, the sight of so much neglect was a hard thing for her to abide.

Setting her jaw against her client's poor management of his land, Sam turned onto the pitted road beneath the warped and faded sign and headed for the barn she could see in the distance.

An S-600 Mercedes sedan was parked at an odd angle to the barn, its silver-and-chrome body catching the sunlight and shooting it back, nearly blinding Sam. As she drew nearer, she saw a man pacing between the car and the barn. At the sound of her truck, he stopped and turned, watching her approach from behind a pair of dark sunglasses. Dressed in a gray pinstriped suit, he seemed at odds with the rustic setting around him...but well matched to the sleek, expensive car parked in front of him.

The dark scowl he wore sent a shiver down Sam's spine. She quickly shoved back the dread of having to deal with him, and forced herself to focus instead on the animal that needed her care. Anxious to get to her patient, she parked and hopped down from the cab of her truck, pausing to grab her vet bag from the toolbox in back. "Nash Rivers?" she asked as she approached him.

He continued to scowl at her. "Yes?"

"I'm here to see about your horse."

Nash slipped his sunglasses to the end of his nose and peered down at her. "*You're* the vet?"

He wasn't the first client shocked to discover that Dr.

Sam McCloud was a woman, but his skeptical tone made Sam tense defensively. "Yeah. You got a problem with that?"

Problem? Nash took his gaze on a slow journey from the top of her sweat-stained gimme cap, over her faded T-shirt and ragged jeans, down to the scuffed toes of her manure-caked boots. Yeah, he had a problem, all right, but it wasn't with her choice of profession. It was with *her*.

She dressed like a down-on-his-luck cowboy and carried a chip on her shoulder the size of a Texas armadillo. She was gruff, mannish and about as charming as a coiled rattler. If a man could get past all that, Nash supposed he might notice the long brown ponytail that poked through the back opening of her cap, and a pair of piercing brown eyes that screamed a silent warning: "One step closer, buster, and I'll jerk your heart out of your chest with my bare hands." And if the look wasn't enough to scare a man off, Nash supposed a fellow might wonder about the figure concealed beneath that oversize T-shirt and baggy jeans.

But not Nash. He wasn't interested in women. Especially one who took such pains to hide her femininity.

"Not as long as you can do your job," he replied tersely, shoving the sunglasses back into place on his nose.

But not before Sam saw the disapproval in his gray eyes. She glared at his back as he turned to lead the way into the barn, tempted to climb right back in her truck and let him find another vet willing to make a call to his pathetic ranch. But she couldn't. Not when an animal needed her care.

Damping down her anger, she followed him, glancing right and left, taking in the empty stalls, the smell of mildew and wood rot that hung in the air. Though the floor of the alley was raked clean, everything else about the place screamed neglect.

Sam was so absorbed in the squalor of the barn's interior, she nearly plowed into Nash's backside when he stopped before a stall. Catching herself just short of physical contact, she took a hasty step backward and pulled her cap farther down on her forehead, shadowing her heat-reddened cheeks. Nervously wetting her lips, she avoided Nash's gaze and turned toward the stall and the horse inside it. A bay, about fifteen hands high, peered back at her.

The horse did something for Sam that a man rarely could—he made her smile. "Hey there, boy," she whispered, stretching out a slow hand in greeting. "What's wrong with you, buddy?" A velvet nuzzle nudged at her hand and Sam's smile broadened.

"Nothing that a twenty-gauge shotgun wouldn't solve."

Sam whipped her head around at the sarcastic comment, her brow furrowed. "And what's that supposed to mean?"

Nash pulled off his sunglasses and polished them on the lapel of his suit. "I want him put down."

The vet bag slipped from Sam's fingers and fell to the floor, shooting up a puff of dust. "Put down?" she echoed. "But why? What's wrong with him?"

"Nothing." He slid the glasses into the inside pocket of his jacket, then rolled his wrist, glancing at his watch, his expression one of impatience. "How long will this take? I've got to get back to my office."

Sam stared at him in disbelief, not at all sure she had heard him correctly. "Are you asking me to put down a healthy horse?"

He gave his sleeve a sharp snap, then lifted his hand to smooth it over hair as black as midnight. "That's the idea. Now, again, how long will this take?"

Sam felt the blood drain from her face, then rise again as anger pulsed through her body. She stooped and snatched her bag from the floor. "A lifetime," she muttered, straightening. "Specifically, his!" she added with a jerk of her head in the horse's direction. She spun and headed for her truck.

The nerve of the man! she fumed silently. Calling her

all the way out here for a job like this. Sam McCloud *never* put down an animal unless there was nothing medically left to offer, and only then if she felt she was saving the animal from more suffering. Grumbling under her breath about fools and murderers, Sam had almost made it to the barn door when a hand closed over her arm, jerking her back around.

Nash Rivers stood in front of her, his eyes narrowed dangerously. A sense of déjà vu swept over Sam as she remembered another time, another man who'd stopped her in just such a way. Fighting back the memory and the fear, she thrust out her chin. "Get your hands off me."

Nash dropped his hold on her and took an impatient breath. "Look, I don't want to argue with you. I just want this taken care of as quickly as possible. I've already wasted several hours waiting for you to respond to my call. I don't relish having to wait any longer while I try to find another vet willing to come all the way out here."

"That's too damn bad."

Again Sam turned toward her truck.

Again Nash grabbed her arm.

Sam wheeled, her eyes shooting fire.

The look was warning enough. Nash dropped his hand. "Listen, lady," he began, struggling for patience, "I want the horse put down. And I'm willing to pay whatever you ask. Just do it quickly, okay? So both of us can get back to work."

"My work is *saving* horses," Sam snapped. "*Not* killing them."

A muscle twitched in his jaw. "That *horse* you're so determined to save nearly killed my daughter. And I'll be damned if I'll give him a chance to try again. Now are you going to put him down, or do I have to call another vet to handle this for me?"

Before Sam could answer, a whirlwind of white-blond hair, clawing fingers and kicking feet came out of nowhere and attacked her. "You can't kill my horse. I won't let you!" the child screamed as she beat at Sam's stomach and arms.

"Hey! Hold on there a minute." Sam struggled frantically to get a grip on the little girl. Finally managing to close her hands on the child's upper arms, she dropped to her knees in front of her, holding her in place. Though dried blood marked an ugly cut from hairline to eyebrow on the girl's forehead, the injury didn't seem to have affected her strength any. Her body remained rigid as she glared at Sam, her lips pressed tightly together, her cheeks red, her eyes puffy from crying.

In spite of her attack on Sam, the child's concern for her horse placed her a notch or two above Nash Rivers in Sam's estimation. "I'm not going to kill your horse, sweetheart, I promise."

The girl continued to glare stubbornly at Sam. "What's your name?" Sam asked, hoping to put the girl at ease.

"Colby."

"Mine's Sam."

In spite of her resentment, the child sputtered a laugh. "Sam? That's a boy's name."

"And a girl's. Short for Samantha. What's your horse's name?"

The smile melted from Colby's face. "Whiskey, and I'm not letting you kill him."

"I'm not going to hurt him. But your daddy tells me that he hurt you."

"He didn't mean to!" Colby cried, her voice rising in panic. "We were just out riding and something spooked him and he shied. It wasn't his fault! Whiskey would never hurt me." She made two quick swipes across her chest. "Cross my heart and hope to die."

From behind Sam came a disbelieving snort, then Nash was dropping down beside them, pulling his daughter from

Sam's grasp and onto his knee. "So how do you explain the bruise on your back and the cut on your head?"

Colby tipped her face up to her father's, her blue eyes brimming. "But, Daddy, I told you that wasn't Whiskey's fault. I fell! He didn't throw me."

Nash stood, placing his daughter firmly back on her feet. "The results are the same," he said, unmoved by her tears. "Now go on back to the house and let Nina tend to your scrapes."

Colby planted her fists on her hips. "No! And you can't make me!" She darted away before Nash could stop her and ran down the alleyway to Whiskey's stall. Hitching a boot onto the bottom rail, she quickly scaled the gate and dropped down on the other side.

"Damn!" Nash muttered under his breath. "Now look what you've done," he said, turning his anger on Sam. "If you'd put the horse down like I asked you, we could have avoided this emotional scene."

Though Sam disagreed—and was tempted to get while the getting was good—something kept her in place. Maybe it was because she saw in Colby a bit of herself at the child's age. Maybe it was because she'd also gone up against her own father—and lost more battles than she cared to remember. Or maybe it was simply because she was afraid that if she left, Nash would find another vet to do his dirty work for him. Whatever the reason, Sam dug in her boot heels. "You'll break her heart if you dispose of her horse."

Nash raked his fingers through his hair, turning the neatly combed style into dark spikes as he looked down the alleyway in the direction Colby had disappeared. "Yeah, but I'd rather break her heart than see her hurt by that beast."

Sam lifted a shoulder. "Accidents happen. She could injure herself just as easily stepping off a curb as she could riding her horse."

He turned to frown at her. "Thanks for the comforting words," he replied dryly.

"I'm not trying to offer comfort. I'm stating facts. I've been riding horses since I was old enough to walk, and I can tell you right now I've hurt myself a lot more often walking than I ever have riding."

"Doesn't say much for your coordination, does it?"

Sam refused to let the barb penetrate. "She needs to have that cut on her head cleaned."

Nash snorted. "I tried. She won't let me touch her."

"That's certainly understandable."

Nash snapped his head around, his eyes like flint as they scraped against Sam. She shrugged, refusing to let him intimidate her. "She's more worried about her horse's welfare than her own. As long as she feels she has to protect him from you, she isn't going to let you near him *or* her."

"So what do you suggest I do? Wait for her to collapse before I seek medical attention for her?"

In spite of his sarcasm, Sam saw the worry in the deep lines plowed between his brows, the concern for his daughter in his tightly compressed lips, in the depths of his gray eyes. That he loved Colby was obvious, that he was overreacting to an accident even more so.

But Sam figured if that cut on the kid's head was going to get tended to, it would be up to her. She heaved a resigned sigh. "Stay here and I'll see what I can do." She strode down the alleyway and stopped in front of Whiskey's stall. Propping her foot on the lowest rung, she draped her arms along the top of the gate. Colby stood inside the stall at the horse's head, stroking Whiskey's nose.

"Go away," she grumbled. "Whiskey and me don't need you."

"I think you do," Sam replied softly. When Colby whipped her head around to glare at her, Sam added, "I've already told you that your horse is safe with me. I would never put down a healthy animal.''

The battle waged within was obvious on the child's face as she struggled to decide whether or not she should trust Sam. She narrowed an eye. "Swear?''

Sam quickly swiped a finger across her heart, just as Colby had done earlier. "Cross my heart and hope to die.''

"Then why are you still here?''

"I thought you might need my services.''

Colby wrinkled her nose. "For what?''

"Well, Whiskey doesn't need any doctoring, but you sure do.''

Colby touched a small finger to the cut on her forehead, frowning. "Daddy wanted to take me to the hospital.''

Sam stretched her neck over the gate, pretending to study the cut. "Doesn't look that bad to me. A little cleaning, some antibiotic ointment, a bandage and you ought to be just fine.''

Colby peered at Sam suspiciously. "I thought vets just doctored animals.''

"Normally they do. But I've doctored some humans, too. In fact, one of my most frequent patients is my nephew, Jaime. He's always getting bummed up in one way or another.''

Colby took a step closer. "This isn't a trick, is it, so you can drug me, then kill my horse?''

Sam had to fight back a laugh at the extent of the child's wild imagination, but she solemnly held up her hand, thumb tucked into palm. "On my honor.''

Colby scuffed the rest of the way to the gate. "Okay, but Daddy has to go, too, or no deal. I don't trust him for a minute.''

This time Sam couldn't stop the laugh. She didn't trust Nash Rivers either. She swung the gate wide and Colby stepped through.

"This isn't going to hurt, is it?" Colby asked, peering up at Sam, her fear obvious.

Sam closed the gate, her smile softening. "It'll sting a little, but that's all. I promise."

"What's going on?" Nash asked impatiently as he joined them.

Colby eased closer to Sam's side, slipping her hand into Sam's. The trust in the gesture touched Sam's soul, but it was the stubborn thrust of Colby's chin when she looked up at her father that rubbed a raw spot on Sam's heart, reminding her of times when she'd stood up against her own father in just such a manner.

"Sam's going to doctor my cuts and you have to go with us."

Nash quickly shifted his gaze to Sam, his surprise obvious. "She is?" At Sam's nod, he let out a sigh, one more of relief than frustration this time. "There's a first-aid kit at the house. If you'll come with me."

Unlike the barn, the house Nash led them to was in good repair. Built of native limestone, the structure looked as if it had stood a century or more and could probably weather another one or two. A covered porch extended across the front of the house and down one side. Wisteria climbed the posts and twined around the railings, its branches dripping with fragrant pink blooms. Behind the veil of leaves, Sam could see two wooden rockers swaying in the afternoon breeze.

She tried to picture Nash sitting there in the evening, slowly rocking, maybe even whittling, while watching the sun set. But the image just wouldn't form. It was easier to imagine him in a boardroom, his feet propped on his desk, phone tucked between shoulder and ear, while a flock of secretaries darted about at his bidding. With a shake of her head, she climbed the steps after him and followed him into the house.

The country-style kitchen they entered reminded Sam a

bit of the one in her own family's home, though the McClouds' was more spacious and had more modern conveniences. Still, it was warm and inviting, with a round oak table scarred from years of use. Sam stooped to pick Colby up and set her on the counter by a chipped porcelain sink while Nash dug through cabinets, looking for the first-aid kit.

Tearing off a strip of paper towel, Sam wet it, then dabbed at the cut, cleaning away the dried blood and dirt. To her relief, she saw that the wound was only superficial, as she'd first thought. "This isn't very deep," she assured Colby with a pat on her knee. "You won't feel much of a sting at all."

Dubiously, Colby watched as Sam opened the first-aid kit Nash had laid out and selected the items she'd need. Nash eased closer to her side, watching, too. Uncomfortably aware of his presence and wishing Colby hadn't insisted on her father being there, Sam gave Nash's shoulder an impatient bump. "Give me some room," she grumbled.

Obediently, Nash stepped back while Sam poured hydrogen peroxide on a cotton ball, but he closed the distance right back up when Sam touched the cotton to Colby's forehead. When Colby cried out, shrinking away, Nash grabbed Sam's hand. "You're hurting her," he growled.

Sam froze as his fingers closed painfully over hers, her breath locked up in her lungs. Images pushed at her from the past, ugly and debilitating. Breathe, she ordered herself sternly, as the familiar panic set in. In, out. In, out. Just breathe, for God's sake!

Colby giggled, unaware of Sam's level of distress. "She didn't hurt me, Daddy. It was just cold."

Nash slowly loosened his grip on Sam. "Oh," he mumbled in embarrassment. "Sorry."

Sam's breath came out in a rush of air. She dropped the cotton ball, then flexed her fingers for a moment as if to rid them of the feel of him. Firming her lips to hide their trembling, she picked up the tube of ointment and squirted a dime-sized dollop onto the tip of her finger. She leaned closer, combing Colby's hair out of the way, and gently traced the wound.

"The cut's a little deeper at her hairline, so I'm going to put on a butterfly bandage to close it in order to prevent scarring."

"Scarring?" Before Sam could stop him, Nash had wedged himself between her and Colby, his face going pale as he examined the wound.

His reaction confirmed Sam's earlier opinion that Nash Rivers was an overprotective father who was overreacting to a simple accident.

"Nothing to worry about," she assured him. "In a couple of weeks, you won't even know it was there." She waited until he moved out of her way, then she carefully stretched the bandage over the skin, closing the wound. "There!" She stepped back, briskly dusting her hands together. "All done." She grinned at Colby. "That wasn't so bad, now was it?"

Colby smiled back shyly. "Not bad at all. You've got soft hands."

Stunned, Sam opened her palms and looked down at them. Soft? Her hands went places Colby wouldn't even want to think about and were as rough as cobs due to the number of washings they received each day.

"I think she means gentle," Nash offered.

Sam whipped her head around to find him watching her. Quickly, she stuffed her hands in her pockets and took another step back, her face flaming as she turned her gaze on Colby. "Speaking of hands, you need to wash yours. We don't want you spreading any germs if you happen to touch your bandage."

"My hands aren't dirty," Colby argued. "I just—"

Nash caught her under the arms and set her on the floor, interrupting her. "Wash them anyway. Doctor's orders.

And stop by Nina's room and apologize for your behavior. You almost gave her a heart attack.''

''Oh, Daddy,'' Colby whined, ''Nina's a worrywart. You know that.''

''She worries because she loves you. Now scoot,'' he ordered firmly, giving her a light swat on the behind to get her moving.

Dragging her feet, Colby obeyed.

And Sam wished she could call her back, for now she was alone with Nash. Fishing for something to say to fill the silence, she asked, ''How long's Colby been riding?''

''Since she was three. She's always been nuts about horses. After we moved to Austin, I found a stable where she could continue her lessons, but it's a forty-five-minute drive from here, so we had to quit after a few months.''

''We?'' Sam asked, cocking her head to look at him. ''You took lessons, too?''

His eyebrows shot up at the question. ''Me? Hell, no! But somebody had to drive her there.''

In other words, Colby's lessons didn't fit into Nash's busy schedule, Sam concluded. ''Would you mind if I saddled Whiskey and rode him around for a bit?''

His frown returned. ''For what purpose?''

''Just to form an opinion. Then I'd like to see Colby ride him, to see how she handles him.''

Nash narrowed his eyes and stabbed a finger in the direction of Sam's chest. ''*You* can ride him all you want, but Colby stays on the ground. I won't have my daughter on that horse's back again.'' He tightened his jaw as he turned to stare down the hallway Colby had disappeared into. The image of her lying on the ground, blood spurting from the wound on her head, formed in his mind and he had to swallow back the fear that rose with it. ''She's my baby,'' he murmured, ''and all I've got left. I can't take a chance on losing her, too.''

* * *

Grateful that Nash had stayed behind at the house to make phone calls, Sam took the saddle Colby had offered her and tossed it onto the horse's back. She settled it over the pad before dipping her knees to reach underneath for the girt. "Did you pick out this saddle yourself, Colby?"

Perched on top of the stall gate, watching, Colby shook her head. "No. Daddy bought it for me for my birthday."

And money was obviously no object, judging by the quality of the leather and the tooled name of the saddle maker. "How old are you?"

"Six. My birthday was May first."

"Really?" Sam tightened the cinch, then threaded the strap back through, making a loop, and tugged it into place. "Mine's the tenth."

"Did you have a party? I didn't get to have one this year. Daddy said he didn't have time to fool with it. But he said next year we'll have a bi-i-ig blowout. Course I don't know who I'll invite. We'll be gone by then."

Sam angled her head, hearing the disappointment in the girl's voice. "You're moving?"

Dejected, Colby dropped her elbow to her knee and her chin onto her palm. "Into a condo, just as soon as Daddy gets the deal on the ranch. He's turning it into a subdivision. You know, houses and shops and stuff. The works. I think he calls it a planned community." She flapped a hand, scrunching her nose. "Or something like that."

"So your daddy doesn't ranch?"

Colby sighed, obviously disappointed. "No. He's a developer. He buys land, divides it all up, builds streets and stuff then sells it to builders."

Which explained to Sam the neglect she'd seen upon first entering the ranch. Nash Rivers wouldn't spend time or money on fences and cultivation if he was planning to subdivide the property for development.

She frowned, remembering the rusted sign that she'd driven under proclaiming the place Rivers Ranch. At one time, someone named Rivers had ranched the land. If not Nash, then who? "Have y'all lived here long?" she asked, her curiosity getting the better of her.

"About a year. We lived in San Antonio when I was little, but when my grandpa died, we moved here."

His father's ranch, then, not Nash's. Probably an inheritance, Sam decided.

"Before we lived in San Antonio, we lived in Dallas," Colby added. "Daddy didn't like Dallas after my mother died. He said it held too many memories, so we moved to San Antonio."

That the child could speak so matter-of-factly about her mother's death surprised Sam. She'd lost her own mother when she was barely two, and though she didn't remember her, she never thought of her without feeling a swell of tears.

"How old were you when your mother died?" she asked softly.

"About eight hours. She was a diabetic. She wasn't supposed to have any babies, but Daddy said she wanted me so bad that she was willing to give up her own life just so that I could be born. That's pretty cool, isn't it?"

The tale was heartbreaking, and made even more so by the emotionless way in which Colby told it. Sam had to ease her breath out before she could answer. "Yeah, that's pretty cool."

"Daddy says I look like her, but I've got her picture in my room on my nightstand and I don't think we look anything alike. Except for the color of our hair, maybe. She was blond like me, but her hair was straight and pretty and mine's all kinky and curly." Wrinkling her nose, Colby wadded a fistful of hair in her hand then let it drop in disgust. "Daddy says it would probably look better if I'd put a comb through it sometimes, but, heck, it just gets tangled up all over again."

Sam bit back a grin as she bent over to lift Whiskey's

front hoof to clean it out. Did the kid ever run out of breath?

"Anyways," Colby went on, with a dismissing wave of her hand, "Daddy loved my mother a lot and sometimes I can tell he still misses her. Are you married?"

The question came out of nowhere and caught Sam off guard. "W-well, no," she stammered as she dropped Whiskey's hoof and moved to pick up his rear one.

"How come?"

Sam felt heat creep up her neck. She bent her head over her work, digging the hoof pick under a clump of dirt and stone. "I don't know. Too busy doctoring horses, I guess."

Colby grinned, showing off the gap where her front tooth should have been. "Maybe you could marry my daddy. He's always telling me I need a mother."

Whiskey's hoof slipped from Sam's grasp. *Mother?* She hauled in a steadying breath and moved to the opposite side of the horse, out of sight of Colby. "I don't think so, sweetheart. Your daddy would probably like to do his own choosing."

"Oh, he wouldn't care. He usually lets me have pretty much what I want, anyway."

And Sam didn't doubt that for a minute. Biting back a smile, she replied, "That may be true, but your daddy needs to do the choosing, just the same." Before Colby got any more ideas in that pretty little head of hers, Sam quickly exchanged Whiskey's halter for a bridle. "Where do you warm him up?" she asked, hoping to put an end to the discussion.

Colby hopped down from the gate. "There's an arena out back. Well, not an arena, really. My grandpa used it to work cattle, but it's big and I've got barrels set up for practicing, so I call it an arena."

Sam chuckled, pausing to ruffle the girl's hair. The child talked a mile a minute, giving her life history when a simple answer would suffice. "Okay, then. Let's head for the arena and we'll see what Whiskey can do."

Once outside, Sam used an old feed bucket as a step to mount the horse, while Colby climbed onto the fence. There was no way Sam's long legs would bend enough to fit into Colby's stirrups, so she simply let her feet dangle at the horse's sides.

Whiskey danced a bit at the unaccustomed weight, then settled down to a walk. Making smooching noises at the horse, Sam eased him into a trot, circled the arena a few times, then ordered him to lope. The horse responded easily to each change of command. Pleased, Sam reined him to a fast stop, then made him back up a few steps.

She grinned over at Colby. "Nice horse."

Colby beamed. "Thanks. Are you going to run the barrels?"

Though she hadn't run a barrel pattern in years, the temptation was too much for Sam. "Do you mind?"

"Heck, no! Whiskey's fast, though, so you better be ready to turn and burn!"

Sam laughed at the barrel-racing term as she guided the horse into position. Drawing a bead on the first barrel, Sam blanked everything else out. Beneath her, she felt the anticipation build in Whiskey. That he was a competitor was obvious in the quiver of muscle, the increased tension on the reins, the tossing of his head. Already seeing herself running the pattern, Sam squeezed her legs against the horse's sides. He bolted forward and she had to keep a tight rein to keep him from getting away from her.

Wind ripped her cap off her head just before they reached the first barrel and sent it spinning behind them. Preparing for the turn, Sam shifted her weight, while sliding her hand down the rein and squeezing her right leg against the horse's side.

Whiskey responded immediately, rating himself for the turn and digging into the freshly plowed earth with his rear hooves. He came out of the first turn and raced for the second. Subconsciously, Sam noted the smooth lead change, the bunching of finely honed muscles and the burst of power as he wrapped the second and headed for the third.

Grinning from the sheer pleasure of it all, she turned the last barrel and gave Whiskey his head as he raced for home. Bracing a hand against the saddle horn, she reined him to a dust-churning stop, then tossed back her head and laughed.

"Wow, Sam! You're good!" Colby called out.

"Whiskey's a good horse," Sam replied, turning him toward the fence where Colby waited.

"He ought to be. I paid enough for him."

Sam's smile slowly wilted as she realized that Nash had joined his daughter at the fence. He stood with one foot propped on the lowest rail, his arms braced along the top one. He'd removed his jacket and tie while at the house and rolled his shirtsleeves halfway up his forearms, revealing tanned skin and a smattering of dark hair. The wind played with his razor-cut hairstyle, blowing a tuft of it across his forehead. The result was a combination of mouthwatering maleness and little-boy charm.

Maybe you could marry my daddy. He's always telling me I need a mother.

Remembering Colby's words, Sam swallowed hard as she met Nash's gaze.

"You've obviously ridden barrels before," he commented.

Gray eyes watched her, measuring her while he waited for a response. Self-consciously, Sam tucked a loose lock of hair behind her ear. "I started when I was about Colby's age and quit when—well, when I went away to college."

"So what do you think of Whiskey?"

Uncomfortable meeting his gaze, Sam ducked her head and leaned forward to scratch the horse's ears. "He's a good horse. Well-trained, even-tempered, but a competitor. The bit might be part of the problem. He seems to fight it a little. A combination might suit him better.'' She lifted her head. "But before I can offer an opinion on whether he's well matched with Colby, I'll need to see her ride.''

Colby twisted around on the fence, her hands pressed together prayerfully at her chest. "Can I, Daddy? Please? I promise I won't fall off this time.''

Nash eyed her, scowling. "I've already told you, Colby. I don't want you on that horse.''

"But Sam rode him and he didn't act up. I promise I'll be careful and besides, you're right here if anything should happen. Please, Daddy? Pretty please?''

How anyone could deny those brimming baby blues, that angelic face, Sam didn't know. The child was obviously a charmer, and knew all the right buttons to push to get what she wanted from her father. But Nash stood firm.

"I said no, Colby.''

Tears that had brimmed, now spilled over. "But, Daddy,'' she cried. "We made a deal. You said if I agreed to move to Austin and leave all my friends in San Antonio, that I could have my very own horse. And now you won't even let me ride him.''

Sam watched Nash's shoulders sag in defeat. It seemed a little guilt heaped on his shoulders accomplished what Colby's sugarcoated pleas couldn't.

"Oh, all right,'' he said grudgingly. "But no running.'' He wagged a finger beneath her nose. "You break a slow lope and you're on the ground, understand?''

Colby's tears disappeared as quickly as they'd formed. "Yes, sir!'' She scrambled down from the fence while Sam slid from Whiskey's back.

Cupping her hands, Sam bent over to boost Colby up. After giving the horse a fond pat on the rump, Sam stepped back out of the way. "Let her rip, cowgirl.''

Laughing, Colby guided the horse to the starting position

again. Sam folded her arms beneath her breasts and watched. She could feel Nash's gaze on her back and tried her best to ignore him. "Remember, Colby," she called. "Easy fingers. Use your legs. And don't let him get ahead of you."

With a salute, Colby fixed her attention on the first barrel. Her expression turned intense as she prepared for the run. Sam felt her own heart thrumming against her ribs and she discreetly crossed two fingers against her forearm, out of Nash's view. "Just stay in the saddle, Colby," she whispered under her breath. "And I'll take care of the rest."

Sam watched Colby ride, making mental notes of the girl's movements as she guided the horse through the pattern. She's leaning forward too much on the barrels, Sam thought. She needs to lean back and tuck her bottom more. And, whoa, that pocket! Way too wide. She needs to tuck his nose more and shape him on the turns.

Colby rounded the last barrel and headed home, her white-blond hair flying out behind her. A smile split her face, revealing that missing front tooth. Sam found her own smile growing. "That was good, Colby. Really good." She caught Whiskey's reins and reached up to give the child a pat on the knee. "You're a natural. No doubt about it."

Colby lifted her head, her eyes shining brightly. "Did you hear that, Daddy? Sam says I'm a natural!"

"Yeah, I heard her."

The voice came from directly behind her and Sam's shoulders tensed as Nash moved up beside her. She smoothed a hand along the horse's neck, trying her best to level her breathing. "The two are well matched," she offered hesitantly. "An adjustment or two in tack will help, but Colby needs more instruction."

Nash stuffed his hands into pockets and rocked back on his heels, his relief obvious. "Well, that pretty much solves it then, doesn't it?"

Sam stole a glance at him. "What do you mean?"

He lifted a shoulder. "I've already told you that the only classes I could find for her are forty-five minutes away and I can't commit to that much time away from work."

"But, Daddy—"

Sam placed a hand on Colby's knee to quiet her. "What if someone came here to teach her?" she asked. "Would you agree to lessons then?"

Nash frowned at Sam. "And how am I supposed to find someone willing to come all the way out here to teach her when I can't even find a place within driving distance to take her?"

Sam glanced up at Colby, shooting her a wink as she squeezed the child's knee in encouragement. "I might know someone who'd be willing to make the drive." She turned her gaze on Nash. "If I can arrange it, would you give Whiskey and Colby another chance?"

Sam could tell that he wanted to say no, but she also knew that she'd trapped him, and he was as aware of that fact as she was. How could he refuse now, when she was practically serving up a teacher for his daughter on a silver platter?

"And who is going to want to take the time to drive out here for a private lesson with one student?" he asked dryly.

Sam met his gaze squarely. "I am."

Two

"*You* are going to give barrel-racing lessons?"

Sam hunched her shoulders defensively. "I'm qualified," she muttered and started around her sister.

Mandy flattened a hand against Sam's chest, stopping her, then leveled a finger at Sam's boots. Grumbling, Sam backed up a couple of steps, hooked a heel in the bootjack by the back door and levered off first one boot then the other.

Satisfied, Mandy stepped aside and went back to the sink where she was peeling potatoes for their dinner. "Yes, you're qualified, but you also have a veterinary practice that keeps you running from one end of the county to the other. How on earth will you ever find time?"

Sam padded across the kitchen to the refrigerator. "I'll make time. If I don't, her daddy'll have her horse put down."

Mandy whirled, her eyes wide. "He wouldn't!"

"That's what he said." Sam one-hipped the door closed

and carried the jug of milk to the counter. "The horse threw her. Or so he says. Colby insists she just fell off." Grabbing a glass, Sam filled it with milk, then reached for a brownie from the pan cooling on a rack.

Mandy slapped her hand away. "You'll ruin your dinner."

Sam had to smile. Though they were only separated by a year in age, at times Mandy acted more like a mother to Sam than a big sister, and even more so since Mandy had married. "Don't worry. I promise I'll clean my plate." She snatched a brownie before Mandy could stop her and took a healthy bite, ignoring Mandy's disapproving frown. "Anyway," she continued around a mouthful of the gooey chocolate, "I have two months to prove to him that his daughter can handle the horse, or else the horse goes."

"Who is this guy? Simon Legree?"

Though Sam was tempted to agree with her sister's assessment of Nash Rivers, she had to be honest. "No, just an overprotective father. His name's Nash Rivers. Ever heard of him?"

Mandy paused in her peeling as she stared out the window, running the name through her mind. She lifted a shoulder and went back to her peeling. "No, but then if he's new to the area, I probably wouldn't."

Sam turned her back to the counter, leaned against it and took a sip of her milk. "They moved here about a year ago from San Antonio. Nash inherited his father's ranch, but plans to divide up the land and sell it."

Mandy nodded sympathetically. "That's happening more and more often. People are having a hard time making a living at ranching."

"Judging by the looks of the place, I'd say he didn't even give it a try. It's going to break the kid's heart when she has to move."

Mandy turned her head slowly to peer at Sam. "You sure seem to know a lot about these people."

Sam snorted a laugh. "Thanks to Colby. The kid could talk the hair off a dog." She shook her head, remembering. "She even suggested that I marry her daddy so that she could have a mother."

Mandy chuckled, then sobered when Sam narrowed an eye at her. "Sorry," she murmured. "I just had this mental image of you changing diapers."

"I can change diapers," Sam replied indignantly. "I certainly changed enough of my nephew's to prove that. But thankfully, Colby's long out of the diaper stage."

"How old is she?"

"Six, going on sixteen."

Mandy chuckled, dropping the last potato into the pot. "Interesting assessment."

Sam blew out a breath. "You wouldn't believe this kid. She can carry on a conversation like an adult, yet throw a tantrum that would rival that of a two-year-old."

"And you willingly volunteered to spend time with her?"

Sam frowned. "Yeah." She turned, propping her forearms on the counter, and stared out the window, holding the glass between her hands. "She kind of reminds me a little bit of myself at that age. She's a tomboy and crazy about her horse. You wouldn't believe how she lit in to me when she heard her daddy order me to put him down." Sam chuckled as the image built. "Took all my strength to hold her back. And she lost her mother before she even had a chance to get to know her, just like we did." She stared a moment longer, than gave herself a firm shake. "Not that I intend to serve as a surrogate mother, mind you. I'm just going to help her improve her riding skills so her daddy will agree to let her keep her horse."

Mandy watched Sam, her instincts going on red alert. "What about her dad? What's he like?"

"Nash?" Sam snorted. "He's a suit."

At Mandy's quizzical look, Sam pushed away from the

counter to pace. "You know the type. Brooks Brothers suit, Italian silk tie, Rolex watch, Mercedes. And all business. I bet he even schedules trips to the rest room on his day planner."

Mandy lifted a brow. She'd never known Sam to get this worked up over a man. "Is he handsome?"

"If you like pretty boys. Merideth would love him," she added, using their younger sister's taste in men as a reference point for Mandy.

"So he *is* handsome."

An image formed in Sam's mind of Nash standing at the fence, the wind lifting his carefully combed hair then dropping it carelessly down on his forehead. Sleeves rolled to the elbow, revealing muscled forearms dusted with dark hair. Carved cheekbones, a stubborn jaw. Gray eyes leveled on her, eyes that seemed capable of stripping her down to her most vulnerable core.

A shiver chased along her spine.

"Yeah, I guess," she replied vaguely, dumping the rest of her milk down the drain, her appetite suddenly gone. "I really didn't pay that much attention."

Three days later, Sam was in the barn at Rivers Ranch, saddling Whiskey in preparation for her first lesson with Colby, when she heard a car door slam in the yard. She lifted her head, turning slightly, and bit back an oath when Nash stepped inside the barn. Wearing a navy blazer and khaki pants, he looked as out of place as he had the first time she'd seen him.

"Where's Colby?" he asked.

"In the house, changing clothes."

He glanced at his watch, frowning. "So when do we start?"

"We?" Sam repeated, arching a brow his way as he strode down the alleyway toward her.

His frown deepened. "Yes, we. I intend to be present at every lesson."

"Great," Sam muttered under her breath. She stooped and caught the rear girt, buckling it into place.

He stopped and braced his hands on his hips. "We didn't discuss the details of this arrangement, so I think we need to do so now. How much are you charging for these lessons?"

"Nothing. I'm doing this for Colby."

His eyes widened then narrowed. "Colby isn't a charity case. I paid her last teacher forty dollars an hour. I'll pay you the same, plus an additional ten dollars for the trip out."

"Keep your money. I don't want it or need it. Like I said, I'm doing this for Colby." She stooped and picked up Whiskey's hoof. "Who's your farrier?"

"Cletus Boggs. Now, about your fee—"

"Better call him. This rear shoe is loose. And tell Cletus to use shoes with rims for the front hooves. It'll help give Whiskey more traction on the turns."

"Fine. And I'm paying you, whether you like it or not."

Sam dropped the hoof and picked up a currycomb, taking out her frustrations with Nash on the burrs matted in the horse's tail. "Your money would be better spent on repairing Whiskey's stall. There are some loose boards he could injure himself on. And you need a new load of shavings for the floor."

"Is that an order or a suggestion?"

The challenge in his voice had Sam cocking her head to look at him. Seeing the hostility in his gray eyes, she tightened her fingers on the comb. "Take it however you want, but the horse deserves the best care you can give him."

"Hi, Daddy!"

Sam and Nash both turned at the sound of Colby's voice. Nash's frown disappeared as Colby skipped down the alleyway toward them. "Hey, sunshine!" He held out his arms and she ran the last few steps and vaulted into them.

Planting a kiss on his cheek, she curled an arm around his neck and reared back to look at him. "Are you going to watch me ride?"

"Yep. Are you ready?"

Colby's mouth puckered into a pout. "I've been ready for hours, but Sam made me go back to the house and put on jeans."

Nash shot Sam a questioning glance. She lifted a shoulder as she dropped Whiskey's tail, then tossed the currycomb back in the bucket. "She had on shorts. I was afraid the saddle would rub sores on her legs."

Nash turned his gaze on his daughter. "Sam's the boss. What she says goes."

He couldn't have said anything that would have surprised Sam more. From the moment he'd announced his intention of being present at the lessons, she'd prepared herself to have to fight him at every turn. Not trusting this unexpected display of support, she eyed him warily. "We're burning daylight," she mumbled. "Let's get started."

Nash swung Colby onto the saddle, then untied the reins and led the horse out into the arena. Sam followed, pulling her cap lower on her forehead to shade her eyes from the bright sunlight.

"Okay, Colby, let's warm him up," she instructed, anxious to get the lesson underway. "Circle the arena a couple of times at a walk, then have him trot. And I want to see you use your body to give him the change of command. Understand?"

Colby beamed at Sam as she took the reins from Nash. "Yes, ma'am."

Sam positioned herself in the middle of the arena, placing herself as far from Nash as possible, while still being able to keep an eye on Colby. Out of the corner of her eye, she saw him at the fence, shrugging out of his jacket. As he leaned to hook it on a fence post, the stretch of starched white cotton across his back revealed muscles that Sam would have preferred not to have noticed. But she did notice and, as hard as she tried, she couldn't seem to tear her eyes away. With his back still to her, he cocked a hip slightly, then lifted a hand and unbuttoned a cuff. He carefully folded the sleeve back two turns, then lifted the opposite hand and started on the other. As each turn revealed another three inches of bare skin, Sam's mouth grew dryer and dryer until it was as parched as the ground beneath her feet.

Ignore him, she told herself, and turned away. Determined to do just that, she folded her arms beneath her breasts and focused on Colby. "Okay, move him up to a trot," she called out.

Colby leaned forward, lifting the reins, and repeated the voice command. Sam nodded her approval, turning slowly in a tight circle as she monitored Colby's movements around the arena...and nearly jumped out of her skin when she made a complete circle and Nash's chest filled her field of vision, inches from her face and blocking her view of Colby. Unaware that he'd even moved, she cried, "What are you doing?"

He lowered his gaze to hers, one brow arched higher than the other, then glanced back over her head toward his daughter. "Watching."

Sam huffed a breath and took a step back, stuffing her hands into her back pockets. "Watch somewhere else. You're in my way."

"It's a big arena. I'd think there's ample room for two adults to watch without any trouble."

"Fine," she snarled. "You can stay here. I'm moving." She stalked off, headed for the far end of the arena...and could've sworn she heard Nash chuckle. The idea that he would laugh at her made her that much more angry. "Okay, Colby," she said irritably, "lope."

Whiskey responded immediately, charging forward. "Slow him down," Sam yelled. "This is a lope, not a race."

Colby dutifully obeyed, giving the reins a sharp tug, and Whiskey settled into a slow lope. Sam nodded her approval as she hitched a boot on a rail behind her. She tucked her fingers into her front pockets and settled her shoulders against the fence. Nash stood where she'd left him, his hands braced on his hips, his dress shirt a shocking white compared to the faded barn behind him. A little too white, Sam decided. A slow, devious smile chipped at one corner of her mouth.

"Take him to the middle, Colby," she ordered, "and give me a fast stop."

Dust churned as Colby swung Whiskey around, then rose into a cloud when the horse slid to a stop on his haunches inches from where Nash stood.

Choking on dust and fanning the air in front of his face, Nash sputtered, "Darn it, Colby! Didn't you see me standing here?"

Colby's chin quivered. "I was just doing what Sam told me to do. You *did* say that she was the boss."

Nash turned to glare at Sam, and though she tried her best not to smile, she failed miserably. Serves him right, she told herself, for being so darn stubborn.

Brushing at the dust on his shirtfront, Nash shifted his gaze back to Colby. "Well, next time, look where you're going."

"I'm sorry, Daddy."

He heaved a deep breath, then lifted a hand to pat her knee. "That's okay, sweetheart. I know you didn't do it on purpose."

Enjoying herself immensely, Sam shouted, "That was a good stop, Colby. Now let's see some figure eights. Trot him once through the pattern so you can show him what you want him to do, then lope. Remember to keep his nose tucked to the center and use your legs to keep him shaped.''

Sam smothered a laugh as she watched Nash jump out of the way, then hustle to the side of the arena as Colby followed Sam's directions.

After a series of seven or more figure eights, Sam instructed Colby to walk Whiskey a couple of laps to cool him off while she set up the barrels. Crossing to the third barrel she tipped it over and rolled it into place. The barrel was old and rusted from years of exposure. As she righted it, she caught a glimpse of Nash watching her, frowning...and another idea occurred to her. ''How about you set the first one,'' she called to him.

Still frowning, Nash gave the barrel closest to him a nudge with his shoe and sent it toppling over. Leaning over, he gave it a shove, rolling it into position, then caught the top rim and levered it upright. Opening his hands, he stared down at the rust and dirt that covered them. He twisted left and right, searching for something to wipe them on.

''What's the matter, Nash?'' Sam mocked. ''Haven't you ever gotten your hands dirty before?''

He turned to scowl at her, then plucked a white handkerchief from his hip pocket and wiped furiously at his hands. Sam tossed back her head and laughed as she headed for the remaining barrel. Whistling happily, she turned it over, gave it a push with her boot and sent it rolling.

Nash watched her, his eyes narrowing. Damn woman! She was trying to make a fool of him, he was sure. ''Well, two can play at this game,'' he muttered under his breath. While Sam was still perched like a pelican, ready to give the barrel another shove, Nash stole up behind her, hooked a foot around the boot that was planted on the ground and gave a sharp tug. Sam yelped, beating wildly at the air in an attempt to regain her balance, but ended up facedown on the ground. She came up spitting dirt, her hands doubled into fists at her sides as she whirled to face Nash.

He smiled sweetly. "What's the matter, Sam? Haven't you ever gotten your hands dirty before?"

"You overgrown juvenile delinquent!" she muttered through clenched teeth.

"Me?" he asked innocently, touching the pad of a finger to his chest. "Isn't that a little like the pot calling the kettle black?" He stepped closer and thumbed a speck of dirt from her face, then left his hand there to cup her cheek. His lips quirked in a teasing smile. "You know, you're kind of cute when you're mad."

Sam felt the blood drain from her face as the pad of each finger, the swell of flesh at the base of his thumb burned into her cheek. Though she expected the familiar panic to set in, she was aware of nothing but the gentleness of his fingers, their underlying strength, and the clear gray eyes that smiled down at her. Heat burned through her and lit a fiery path all the way to her lower abdomen where it settled into a burning pool of fire. The sensation was a rare one for Sam and so unexpected she didn't know what to do with it. Falling back on her anger, she hauled off and took a swing at him.

Nash slapped a hand on her wrist, stopping her fist about three inches from his nose. Eyes and lips that a moment ago had teased suddenly sobered. "I wouldn't do that if I were you," he warned in a low voice. "My mother taught me not to hit girls, but for you I might make an exception."

"Hey, Daddy!" Colby called. "What are you doing to Sam?"

Slowly Nash loosened his grip, and turned Sam's hand over, forcing her palm open. He smoothed the pads of his fingers from her wrist to the tips of her squared nails, his gaze locked on hers. Lightning streaked up Sam's arm at the contact and jump-started her heart, which seemed to have stopped beating.

"Nothing, sweetheart," he said, though he kept his gaze

leveled on Sam. "Just checking to see if Sam cut her hand on that old barrel."

"Are you hurt, Sam?" Colby asked in concern, trotting her horse over to join them.

Sam snatched her hand from Nash's grasp and dragged it across the seat of her pants as she took a step back. That he was aware of his effect on her was obvious from the knowing glint in his eyes. Swallowing hard, she turned, tearing her gaze from his, and forced a smile for Colby's benefit. "No. It was just a scrape." She hauled in a breath to steady her heart. "Are you ready to run some barrels?"

"There's this man."

"Oh?"

After a year of counseling, Sam was used to having her therapist respond to everything she said with a question, but she frowned at the suggestion in this one-word response. "It's not what you think."

Dr. Camille Tilton leaned slightly forward in her chair, folding her hands on her desk, her face expressionless. "And what am I thinking?"

Sam squirmed, already regretting that she'd made this appointment. "That I'm interested in him or something," she mumbled.

Camille leaned back, templing her fingers in front of her. "If he's unimportant, then why do you mention him?"

"Because—well, because he touched me," Sam blurted out.

"Where?"

Sam frowned, rubbing her hands down her thighs, not enjoying being forced to relive the moment. Two days had passed since the event, but Sam could still feel the impression of his fingertips on her cheek. She lifted a hand, demonstrating. "Here."

"And this upset you."

A statement rather than a question this time. Camille

knew Sam well. "Yeah. Well, sort of," she admitted hesitantly. She rolled her eyes heavenward at her inability to put her feelings into words. These sessions were always painful. She sometimes wondered why she subjected herself to them.

Because you want a life, her conscience reminded her, *a normal one.* And if it meant sitting through years of therapy, answering questions, baring her soul, by God she'd have one!

"He made me feel…I don't know, kind of hot and cold at the same time."

"Heat can be associated with anger. Were you angry with him?"

"Yeah. In the beginning, at least."

"And cold can be associated with fear. Was this what you were feeling?"

"Maybe." Sam sat up straighter in the chair, digging her fingers through her hair. "I don't know. I just felt weird."

"Weird. Can you explain that more fully?"

"If I could, I wouldn't be sitting here," Sam said dryly.

An understanding smile softened Camille's face. "Well, let me see if I can help you. Let's talk about fear first. Did his touch frighten you?"

"I always freeze up when a man gets near me. You know that."

"Yes, and the fear is understandable, considering your past. But you said you were angry with him initially. Why don't you tell me about that."

Sam heaved a breath. "I'm giving his daughter riding lessons and he insists on being present during every lesson. He's a suit. You know the type. Manicured nails, not a hair out of place. And he keeps crowding me. Everywhere I turn, he's there."

"And you resent that."

"Yeah," Sam said sourly. "So I decided to teach him a

lesson. You know, in hopes he'd decide to quit hanging around for the lessons.''

''And what did you do?''

Sam smirked, remembering. ''Well, I arranged it so he'd have to eat some dust, get his hands dirty.''

''Couldn't you have just requested that he not attend the lessons?''

Sam snorted. ''He'd never go for that. He's much too protective of Colby. Colby's his daughter,'' she offered in explanation.

Camille merely nodded. ''Let's get back to how you felt when he touched you. You said initially you were angry, which I assume was due to his presence and your not wanting him there for the lesson. Let's focus now on what else you might have been feeling, specifically when he touched you. Are you attracted to him at all?''

Sam felt heat burn her cheeks. Though she was tempted to lie, she knew Camille would see right through her. She always did. ''I don't know. Maybe.''

''Is he handsome?''

''Yeah, I guess, but he's definitely not my type.''

''And what is your type?''

Sam snorted indelicately. ''Definitely not a suit.''

''But something about him appeals to you. If it isn't his appearance, perhaps it is something intrinsic, or something purely physical. A woman can be drawn to a man for reasons other than the way he dresses. In one word, describe him to me.''

''Protective.''

''Of whom?''

''His daughter.''

''Another word.''

''Anal.''

''In what sense?''

''He's always looking at his watch like he's got somewhere to go, some place to be. And he's obsessively neat.''

"In what way?"

"How he dresses. Slacks perfectly creased, starched shirts. And he doesn't like to get his hands dirty."

"Another word."

"Sad."

Camille arched a brow. "Elaborate."

Wishing she'd chosen another word, Sam squirmed. "His wife died after giving birth to his daughter. Colby told me that they moved from Dallas to San Antonio, because there were too many memories there for her dad."

"Sad, then, is Colby's assessment of her father, not yours."

"No," Sam said slowly, only beginning to realize that it was true. "I've seen it, too. When he was telling me he didn't want his daughter to ride her horse anymore, he said the reason was that he was afraid she'd get hurt, and she was all he had left. And when he said it, there was a sadness in his voice that almost bordered on fear."

"So the man has some fears of his own to deal with."

"Yeah, I guess," Sam admitted grudgingly.

"When he touched you, did you want him to remove his hand?"

The quick change in topic took Sam by surprise. "I—I—well, no, not exactly," she finally admitted.

"Was he rough?"

"No. Gentle. Almost tender. It was the heat that scared me."

"His hand was hot?"

"No, warm. The heat was inside me."

"Where?"

Sam placed a hand on her abdomen, feeling the muscles knot again at the memory. "Here. But all over, really."

"Have you had much experience with sexual desire, Sam?"

Again Sam felt heat crawl up her neck to redden her cheeks. She was twenty-nine years old and still a virgin, for God's sake. And because of some jerk who'd thought he could force her to have sex with him, it seemed she was destined to remain one forever. "You know I haven't."

"But you've been attracted to men, haven't you?"

"A few."

"But never enough to allow one to get close to you."

"I couldn't."

"Wouldn't," Camille corrected. "It was a mental decision, not a physical one."

Sam's lips thinned in anger. "With the same result."

"Yes, but the distinction is important." Camille leaned forward again, planting her elbows on her desk and her fists beneath her chin. "When do you and Colby have another lesson?"

"Tomorrow."

"Will her father be present?"

Sam snorted again. "You can count on it."

Camille smiled. "Good. I'd like you to try something. A little experiment, if you will."

Sam narrowed her eyes suspiciously. "What?"

"If during the lesson he places himself near you, don't move away. Force yourself to remain in place. See what other feelings surface. Can you do this?"

Her mouth suddenly dry, Sam tried to work up enough saliva to swallow. "I could try."

Camille smiled. "Wonderful." She flipped open her appointment book. "Why don't we meet again at the same time in two weeks?"

Sam closed her hands over the chair's arms and levered herself to her feet. "Okay. But don't expect anything earth-shattering to have occurred. I just said I'd try."

Camille made the notation in her book, then closed it, rising. She stepped around the desk and put a hand on Sam's shoulder as she walked to the door with her. "That's all I ask, Sam. That you try."

* * *

"The surveyors are finished with their work. I dropped a copy of their report off at Jasco's so they can start laying out the roads. The——" Marty lifted his head and saw that his boss was staring out the window. "Are you hearing a word I'm saying?" When Nash didn't respond, Marty slapped a hand on top of the desk. "Nash!"

Nash started, bumping a knee on the lap drawer of his desk. "What?"

"Jeez," Marty grumbled. "Where were you, anyway?"

Nash straightened, raking a hand though his hair in hopes of scraping the image of Sam McCloud from his brain. "Sorry. I've got a lot on my mind."

"Yeah, so do I. And most of it deals with the Rivers Ranch. Now are you ready to listen?"

"Do you know the McClouds?" Nash asked.

"The ones who own the Double-Cross Heart Ranch?"

"Yeah. Do you know them?"

"Not personally, though I've heard a lot about them."

"Tell me what you know."

"If you're thinking about trying to buy their land, you can forget it. Those people are rooted in deep. That ranch has been in their family since back in the 1800s. Its now owned by the three McCloud sisters. In fact, they just doubled the ranch's size when one of the sisters married."

Nash's ears perked up. "Which sister?"

"The oldest one. Mandy, I think's her name." Oblivious to the relaxing of Nash's shoulders, Marty went on, "Anyway, she married Jesse Barrister and they combined the Double-Cross and the Circle Bar."

"Jesse Barrister? Any relation to Margo Barrister?"

"Stepson. And there's no love lost between them."

Nash frowned. "What about the other sisters?"

"One's an actress. She lives in New York, I think. Appears on some soap opera. My wife's a big fan. Personally, I can't stomach those shows. One catastrophe after another, with everybody switching spouses all the time."

"What about the other sister?"

"Sam?"

"Yeah. What do you know about her?"

"Not much. She's been away at school for years. Became a vet, as I recall. Heard she was coming back here to set up her practice on the family ranch. Those women are tight," he said, chuckling. "You don't mess with one without the other two jumping into the fray. And they're rich, to boot. Old Lucas knew how to make a dollar and turn it into ten. From what I heard, he left them a chunk of cash, plus the ranch."

Which explained to Nash why Sam had said she didn't need his money. But it certainly didn't explain why she was willing to spend time with a six-year-old kid.

"I've hired Sam to give Colby barrel-racing lessons."

"Really?" Marty arched a brow. "I'd say you're damn lucky to get her. She was a contender for the national title at one time. Dropped out when her old man died." He wagged his head. "A shame, too. As I recall, she all but had the title in her hand."

"She seems a little…well, rough around the edges."

Marty slapped his knee, chuckling, obviously enjoying Nash's choice of words. "That'd be Sam, all right. She's a tomboy through and through. She could outride and outrope any boy she went up against. The exact opposite of her sister, Merideth. She's the actress," he said in explanation, then whistled through his teeth. "Now that one is all woman. A real babe."

Though Nash found the contrast interesting, he wanted to know more about Sam. In his opinion, the woman acted a little strange and he didn't entrust his daughter to just anyone. "Colby's safe with Sam, isn't she? I mean there's nothing I should worry about, is there?"

"With Sam? Heck, no! She wouldn't hurt a fly. In fact, it makes sense that she's a vet. She always had this soft spot for any orphaned animal." His forehead suddenly furrowed into a frown. "There was something, years ago," he began, "a rumor of some kind floating around." His forehead pleated as he tried to remember, then he shook his head. "It escapes me now, but I can assure you that Colby is safe with Sam."

After Marty left the office, Nash settled down to work. Plats were scattered across his desk, sharing the space with aerial views of the Rivers Ranch. Thick stacks of bids were propped on one corner, waiting for his consideration, while a prospectus for potential investors served as a coaster for a mug of murky coffee.

The prospectus no longer served any purpose, since Nash already had all the investors he needed to begin the project. The groundwork was all laid. It was just a matter of putting the wheels into motion. If Nash was right—and his gut instincts told him he was—Rivers Ranch would soon become one of the most sought-after developments in the Austin area.

Nash picked up one of the aerial shots and leaned back in his chair to study it. He could see the tin roofs of the old homestead and barn, both a faded red, which were the only outbuildings remaining on the land. There had been other barns in the past, but they had all given way to time and weather, leaving nothing but a scar on the landscape to mark where they'd once stood. Nash remembered one in particular, a dome-shaped structure where hay and grain were once stored.

He remembered well the sweltering summers he'd spent cutting, raking and baling hay on the seat of a bone-jarring tractor, then hauling it to the barn and stacking it for storage. He remembered, too, loading that same hay onto the bed of the old farm pickup in the winter months and hauling it out to the pastures, in freezing rain and biting cold, to keep the livestock from starving.

He shook his head and tossed the picture back to his desk. "Never again," he muttered. Backbreaking, sweat-inducing work with no guarantee of compensation. His grandfather and his father might have enjoyed that kind of life, but not Nash. He'd watched the ranch and its never-ending demands suck the life right out of both men and had sworn that he'd never follow in their footsteps.

When he announced he wanted to go to college and pursue a degree in civil engineering, his father had accused him of being lazy, of wanting a cushy life. But if putting in a ten-hour day in an air-conditioned office and making regular trips to the bank made him lazy, then that was just fine with Nash. He'd had a stomach full of the ranching life before he'd turned eighteen. Give him a white-collar job any day.

Selecting a bid from the top of the stack, he began to study the costs of laying the underground electrical lines. The cost was exorbitant, but Nash considered the end results well worth the cash outlay. The caliber of people he wanted to attract wouldn't want their views of the Texas Hill Country marred by electrical poles and wires.

He already had a couple of doctors interested in buying five-acre tracts and the homes they planned to build were in the half-million to million-dollar range. With the deed restrictions already established within the covenants, their investments would be protected. A golf course and clubhouse, already in the design stage, would attract even more of the white-collar crowd.

Everything was clicking along smoothly, falling neatly into place...with the exception of Colby. Nash frowned as his thoughts took a U-turn to his daughter and her opposition to his plans. Colby didn't want him to cut up the Rivers Ranch and had been very vocal about it.

"And what *isn't* she vocal about?" he muttered to himself. Colby had an opinion on everything and her focus at the present seemed to be on one Sam McCloud. She'd been singing Sam's praises from dawn 'til dusk for three days now and Nash was getting damn sick and tired of hearing the woman's name. It was "Sam this," and "Sam that." Colby had even told Nash she thought Sam was pretty.

Pretty? Nash snorted. If you liked tomboys with an attitude. In his opinion, Sam McCloud was as plain as a vanilla wafer, thin as a rail and dressed like a cowboy. And she was flat-chested to boot! Or at least he thought she was. It was kind of hard to tell what lay beneath those ratty, oversize T-shirts she wore.

Disgusted with himself for even giving her a thought, he forced his attention back to the bid he'd been studying.

"Pretty," he muttered, giving the papers a firm snap. "Pretty bossy, maybe," he added disagreeably.

Three

Two lessons a week with Colby hadn't seemed like that big of a deal when Sam had originally agreed to the schedule. But now she was having second thoughts. Not that Colby was a problem. She was a good kid, eager to learn, and as playful as a pup when the mood suited her.

It was Nash who was giving her the second thoughts...or maybe, more accurately, it was Camille's suggestion of the little experiment with Nash that was giving her second thoughts. Just thinking about it made Sam's hands grow damp on the steering wheel as she turned onto the road leading to the Rivers Ranch.

She knew he'd be there waiting for her. He'd already let it be known that he would be present for every lesson. But how in the heck was she supposed to pull off Camille's ridiculous experiment when every time he got within two feet of her she froze up like an engine without oil? And if he touched her again.... Sam shuddered at the thought. There was no way she could go through *that* again.

She parked in front of the barn and let out a weary sigh. *A life, Sam,* she told herself firmly. You want a life and if it means brushing shoulders with Nash Rivers to get over this ridiculous fear of men, then by God you'll do it! Besides, Camille had only said she had to try.

Her stomach already knotting convulsively, Sam glanced around as she stepped from her truck, but there wasn't a soul in sight. Heat radiated from the hard-packed dirt beneath her boots and worked its way up through the soles, making her feet burn and itch. Tucking a boot behind her thigh, she gave it a brisk rub, but only succeeded in polishing the top, doing nothing to ease her burning feet. With a sigh, she dropped her foot and turned to squint toward the house. Nash's car was parked out front, but there wasn't a sign of him or Colby anywhere. Confident that the two would appear eventually, Sam headed for the barn and its welcoming shade.

Once inside, she paused a moment to let her eyes adjust to the change in light. And that's when she saw him. Nash. Sitting on a bale of hay in front of Whiskey's stall, his face buried in his hands.

The despondent hunch of his shoulders made Sam momentarily forget about the ridiculous experiment. Instinctively, she took a step toward him, then stopped, reluctant to approach him. "Nash?"

He lifted his head and turned to look at her.

A chill chased down Sam's spine and gooseflesh pebbled her arms when she saw the emptiness in his eyes. Sure that something awful had happened, she ran the distance that separated them and dropped to her knees beside him. She wanted to reach out to him, if only to put a concerned hand on his arm, but years of shunning physical contact kept her palms pressed tightly against her thighs. "What's wrong?" she asked as she glanced frantically around. "Where's Colby?"

He braced his hands on his knees and pushed to his feet.

"She's in town with her grandmother," he said miserably.
"There won't be a lesson today," he added. "In fact, there
won't be any more lessons at all."

Slowly Sam rose. "But why?"

"Colby broke the rules. She rode Whiskey this morning
while I was gone."

Sam felt the blood drain from her face. "Is she hurt? Did
Whiskey throw her?"

He waved away her concern. "No. She's fine. It's
Nina." He braced his hands at his hips and turned his face
to the barn's ceiling, his jaw tensing. "She threw a fit when
she discovered that Colby had slipped out of the house to
ride. She called me at work and demanded that I come
home and get rid of the horse."

"Isn't that a bit extreme? Couldn't Colby be punished
in another way?"

"I wish she could, but her grandmother can be pretty
stubborn. And she's right," he conceded reluctantly. "I did
tell Colby that if I caught her on the horse without either
you or me present, the horse would go." He turned, and
Sam saw the rifle propped against the stall door beside him.

"Oh, Nash, you can't!" she cried and took a quick step
sideways, placing herself between him and the gun.

"Don't worry," he said, obviously embarrassed by his
own cowardice. "I thought about it, but I couldn't even
bring myself to point the gun."

Sam breathed a sigh of relief. There might be hope for
Nash, after all. "So what are you going to do?"

"Sell him, I guess. But I'm afraid that'll break Colby's
heart almost as much as if I shot him."

"Let me have Whiskey," Sam said impulsively. "I'll
take him home with me until the dust settles around here,
and you decide what you want to do with him."

He looked at her in surprise. "Would you?"

"Yes." As soon as the word was out of her mouth, Sam
wished she could call it back. She caught her bottom lip

between her teeth, already imagining Colby's reaction when she found her horse gone. And this time, she'd blame Sam, as well as Nash. "When do you expect Colby and her grandmother to return?"

Nash glanced at his watch. "They've been gone almost an hour, so they should be back any minute now."

Which gave Sam no time to make a run to the Double-Cross for her trailer. "I'll need to use your trailer to haul him home."

Nash waved his arm expansively. "Take whatever you need."

Working together, Nash and Sam hooked the trailer to Sam's truck and loaded Whiskey inside. They brushed hands, bumped shoulders, knocked heads, but Sam was so anxious to leave before Colby returned, she didn't even notice the physical contact.

After locking the doors into place behind the horse, Sam turned and found Nash looking at her and all those uneasy feelings returned with a vengeance. Feeling awkward and much too aware of his presence, she stuffed her fingertips into the front pockets of her jeans. "I'll take good care of him."

"I don't doubt that for a minute." He took a step closer and placed a hand on Sam's arm. "I really appreciate your doing this."

Though her first impulse was to shake off his hand, Sam could almost feel Camille's nudge. *Force yourself to remain in place. See what other feelings surface.* It took all her strength and determination to do so, but Sam stood her ground, diligently trying to focus on her emotions rather than the feel of his hand on her.

But Nash's touch was like a brand, the heat crawling up the length of her arm to stain her neck and cheeks, then diving down to swirl low in her abdomen. His eyes, gray and full of emotion, seemed to penetrate her flesh, baring her soul. How was she supposed to think, to analyze, for God's sake, when she could barely breathe?

Unable to stand the torture another second, she stepped back, breaking the contact. "When you decide what you're going to do with him," she said hastily, "let me know."

"I appreciate that. And don't think I expect you to take on the financial responsibilities of caring for him. I'll send a check to pay for his feed and what other expenses might come up."

"Okay." With nothing left to say, Sam turned and strode for her truck.

"Sam?"

She turned, her hand on the door handle.

"Thanks."

The simple word of gratitude sent a warmth rushing through her that she felt all the way to her toes. "No problem." Quickly she climbed inside the cab and started the engine. As she glanced up at the windshield, she saw a car bumping down the rutted road toward the house, chased by a cloud of thick dust. "Oh, no," she murmured, recognizing Colby as the passenger.

Nash must have seen her too, because he slapped a hand against the side of the trailer. "Go!" he yelled, frantically gesturing at Sam. "Get him out of here!"

She quickly shifted into gear and pressed down on the accelerator. But by the time she reached the Y where the road split, one track leading to the barn and the other to the house, Colby was already leaping from the car and racing toward her. At the fear she saw on the child's face, Sam increased the pressure on the accelerator and swallowed back the lump that rose in her throat as she made the sharp turn.

Glancing up into the rearview mirror, she saw Colby running down the road behind her, her hands outstretched, tears streaking down her face. Nash was two steps behind her. As Sam watched, tears burning her own eyes, Nash scooped up his daughter and hauled her up into his arms. With his hand cupped behind her head, he pressed her tear-streaked face to his chest and dipped his head low over hers.

Turning her gaze back to the windshield, Sam gulped back the wad of emotion that plugged her throat. "Don't worry, Colby," she whispered tearfully. "I'll take care of him for you." She dragged a hand beneath her eyes. "Cross my heart and hope to die."

That last scene at the Rivers Ranch played through Sam's mind for days. Nash scooping the heartbroken Colby into his arms and dipping his head low over hers, tears glistening in his eyes. The image was the epitome of what a father's love should be. Compassionate, comforting. Remorseful, for he knew that he was the cause of his daughter's misery. Strong, because he had held fast to his decision to send Whiskey away, knowing that discipline was as important to his daughter as his love.

But the images that played through Sam's mind at night, the ones that spawned her dreams were different. They were of Nash. Only Nash. He was with her in her bed, his arms wrapped tight around her, his body pressed close to hers. He would kiss her, whisper sweet, seductive words in her ear. And because it was a dream, Sam would respond to him. She'd touch him, kiss him, tease him with her lips until he moved over her. She gloried in the feel of his naked flesh rubbing against hers, the swell of his arousal pressing against her femininity. Locked safely in the web of her dream, she would arch to meet him and take him deep inside her where the fires burned the hottest.

But then she would wake up and reality would hit when she found herself alone, with nothing but a yearning that was growing stronger every day. If she was a teenager, she supposed she'd describe her growing infatuation with Nash as a crush. But what would a grown woman label the attraction? Lust?

Probably, she decided, as she climbed into bed. She rolled to her side, plumping her pillow beneath her head. And why not? Nash was gorgeous and sexy as hell. The only problem was, Sam was neither of those things. Why would a man like Nash Rivers bother to look twice at a woman like her? Even if by some twist of fate he *did* notice her and decide to approach her, Sam knew she'd just freeze up—she always did when men got near her.

So what was the point of torturing herself by thinking about him, dreaming about him?

"Because that's all I have," she whispered sadly against her pillow. "And probably all I'll ever have." She closed her eyes, waiting for him to come to her in the hazy cloud of a dream.

"Jesse," Sam ordered, addressing her brother-in-law. "Hand me that pair of wire cutters."

Jesse nabbed them from the tailgate of the truck and passed them to Sam, then knelt down beside her. "Need me to do anything?"

Catching her lower lip between her teeth, Sam swiped at the sweat beading her forehead before angling her hand slightly to slip the cutters between the cow's rear leg and the strand of barbed wire that was wrapped around it. "Just make sure she keeps her hooves on the ground. I've had about all the abuse I can handle for one day."

Jesse chuckled, but braced a hand low on the cow's leg while Pete, the foreman on the Circle Bar, tightened his hold on the rope around the cow's neck. "And who's been abusing my favorite vet?"

Sam made the first snip and carefully began to unwind the wire from the torn flesh. "One of Burt Cornish's goats didn't like the idea of me messing with her baby. Kinda took it personal, I guess. Butted me right square in the behind while I was trying to give her kid her shots.''

Jesse laughed, then winced as a chunk of hair and hide stuck to one of the barbs Sam peeled away. "I swear," he said in disgust, "cows have to be the stupidest animals on this earth. Trying to bust through four strands of barbed wire when she's got over a hundred acres in her own pasture to graze." He shook his head. "Plumb loco, if you ask me."

Sam repositioned the cutters, putting her muscle behind her grip. "You know what they say about the grass always being greener on the other side," she said through clenched teeth. She grunted when the wire gave way and rocked back on her heels. Lifting her forearm again, she dragged it across her forehead before resuming the tedious job of plucking the embedded wire from the flesh.

A horn blasted and Jesse spun around on the balls of his feet. A smile built on his face as he rose, shoving back his hat. "Looks like Mandy's going to pay us a visit. Man, I hope she brought a cooler along. I could sure use a cold one about now. How about you, Pete?"

"I s'pose I could choke down a beer if'n it was offered to me," he said drolly. Pete turned his head in the direction of the approaching truck. "Who's that with her?"

Sam huffed an impatient breath. "Are you two going to help me, or not?"

Jesse braced his hands against his knees, leaning down. "Sorry. What do you need me to do?"

"There's a spray bottle in the back of my truck. Get it, and that yellow jar of ointment while you're at it."

Jesse straightened and moved to the side of the truck to do Sam's bidding. "Hi, sweetheart!" he called as Mandy pulled up beside him and parked.

Mandy swung down from the truck and rose on tiptoe to press a kiss on her husband's waiting lips. Though Sam's attention was centered on the cow's leg, she heard the smack and groaned. "Good grief," she muttered. "Are we going to doctor this cow, or play kissy-face all day?"

Mandy laughed, taking the spray bottle and jar of ointment from her husband. She moved to squat down beside Sam. "Trouble?"

"Yeah." Sam took the bottle and sprayed the cow's leg with disinfectant. "These dang Barrister cattle haven't got the good sense to stay out of barbed wire." She spared her sister a frown as she traded the bottle for the jar. "What are you doing out here?"

"I brought someone to see you."

Sam cocked her head over her shoulder just as Nash rounded the front of the truck. Her eyes widened in surprise, then narrowed. Although she'd received a check from Nash to cover Whiskey's expenses, she hadn't seen him or heard from him in the week since she'd hauled the horse away from Rivers Ranch.

As usual he was dressed to the nines, right down to the shine on his Italian loafers. "What's *he* doing here?" she whispered under her breath.

"He came to the Double-Cross looking for you." Mandy lifted a shoulder as she rose. "Said it was important, so I offered to drive him out." She turned back to the truck, waiting for Nash to join her. "Nash, I'd like you to meet my husband, Jesse Barrister. Jesse, this is Nash Rivers."

The two men shook hands. "Pleased to meet you," Jesse said, smiling.

"Likewise," Nash replied. "I've had the pleasure of meeting your stepmother, Margo. Although, to be honest, she never mentioned any stepchildren."

Listening to the exchange, Pete snorted, then quickly looked away when Jesse shot him a frown. "She wouldn't," Jesse replied dryly, then chuckled. "But then again, I rarely admit to having a stepmother, either. What can I do for you?" he asked cordially.

"Well, actually I came to see Sam."

Her cheeks burning when she felt four pairs of eyes hit her back, Sam dipped two fingers into the ointment and began smearing it on the cow's scraped and torn flesh. "Come to check on Whiskey?" she asked without sparing Nash a glance.

"Partly." A pinstriped knee appeared next to hers as Nash hunkered down beside her. Already hot from spending a day in the sun, Sam's blood turned to near boiling as she felt the heat of Nash's body pulse against hers. "But I wanted to talk to you, too," he added quietly.

Sam's heart shot to her throat and lodged there. He'd come to see her? Could it be possible that he was interested in her? "What about?"

"About giving Colby lessons again."

Quickly Sam rose, swiping the palms of her hands down her jean-clad thighs, feeling like a fool for thinking he'd come to see her. She started gathering her supplies. "Why the change of heart?"

Nash pressed his hands to his knees, rising. "She's been miserable ever since you took him away. Cries constantly."

Sam tossed the supplies into her toolbox and plucked out a stained rag. Wiping her hands, she looked at him over her shoulder. "So you want your horse back?"

Nash stole a glance at Mandy and Jesse. "Well, no," he mumbled. "Not exactly."

Mandy, always sensitive to others' feelings, must have sensed that Nash wasn't comfortable conducting this conversation in front of a bunch of strangers because she looped her arm through Jesse's and tipped her face up to his. "Are y'all through here?" she asked him.

Jesse looked at Sam. "Are we?"

"Yeah." Sam turned to Pete. "You can let her go now. Just keep an eye on her. If you notice any swelling, you'll need to pen her for a few days. If that happens, call me and I'll drop off some antibiotics."

While Pete eased the rope over the cow's head, Mandy

opened the truck door. "Jesse, you and Pete hop in and I'll give you a ride back to the Circle Bar. Sam, you don't mind driving Nash back to the Double-Cross, do you?"

Before Sam could come up with an excuse not to, Pete and Jesse were climbing into Mandy's truck. "Well, no, I guess not," she mumbled disagreeably as she watched the door close behind the three of them. "Get in," she ordered Nash, then climbed behind the wheel and started the engine.

Before he had a chance to close the door fully, she was making a wide U-turn, then heading for the gate that opened onto the highway. Pete stood at the opening, waiting for Sam to drive through before closing the gate behind her. As Sam passed Mandy's truck, she cast a sour look her sister's way. Mandy merely smiled and waggled three fingers.

"Nice family," Nash commented.

"They have their moments."

"You have two sisters, right?"

"Yeah. The other one lives in New York."

"You're lucky. I don't have any brothers or sisters."

"You want one of mine?" Sam asked dryly.

Nash chuckled. "No, but Colby might take you up on that offer. She's always complaining about not having any sisters or brothers to play with."

At the mention of Colby, Sam's frown deepened. "She's taking it pretty hard, huh?"

Nash caught the knot of his tie and gave it a tug. "To say the least." He frowned as he craned his neck to release his shirt's top button. "Nina won't budge on me bringing the horse back, though."

"Who runs your house, anyway, you or this Nina person?"

Nash chuckled, though the sound lacked humor. "Nina, without question." He propped an elbow against the door and laid his index finger along his upper lip, staring at the landscape as it flashed past. "Nina's my wife's mother, not mine," he said after a moment's silence. "After Stacy died, Nina moved in with me to help care for Colby. Since she was a widow and didn't have any other responsibilities, the arrangement suited us both. At least it did for a while. Now—" He dropped his hand, guilt at the disloyal thought making him sit up straighter in the seat. "She means well. She's just—well, she's just overprotective. Which is understandable, I guess, considering Colby's all she has left in the world."

"But Colby's *your* daughter," Sam reminded him firmly. And all that you said you had left in this world, she added, silently. "Not Nina's."

He glanced at Sam then, and his eyes were filled with so much remorse she wished she'd kept her remarks to herself. But it was too late to take the biting words back now.

"Yes, she is." He sighed and turned his gaze to the windshield. "All of this is my fault, really. When my wife died, I was so consumed with my own grief, that I just let Nina take over. The arrangement worked perfectly when Colby was a baby, but when she started walking and talking and demanding more and more freedom, the problems started. Now, more often than not, I find myself caught in the middle, trying to smooth things over between the two. I've considered hiring someone else to care for Colby, but it would kill Nina if I did that. Besides, I need Nina. The thought of Colby being cared for by strangers—well, it isn't something I care to think about."

His explanation gave Sam a pretty good idea of the setup in his home and his affection for his daughter, but didn't sway her opinion much of Colby's grandmother. "She can't keep Colby in a plastic bubble all her life."

"I know that. Or at least I do here," he said, touching a finger to his head. "But Nina can be stubborn, and Colby..." He wagged his head, chuckling ruefully. "Well, you've been around Colby enough to see how she is."

Sam smiled in spite of herself as she braked the truck to a stop in front of the barn on the Double-Cross. "Kinda like two old billy goats going head to head, are they?"

"That would be putting it mildly." He sighed again, twisting around on the seat to look at her. With his leg angled, one knee almost touched Sam's. "I'm just trying to find a way to keep them both happy. Colby wants her horse, but Nina refuses to allow him back on the ranch for fear Colby will sneak off again to ride him...and get hurt."

That knee bothered Sam a bit. The V-shaped view of his crotch worried her more. An image of him naked, as he appeared in her dreams, formed in her mind. She frowned and scooted closer to her door, trying to focus on the conversation rather than that image. "I can see your problem," she muttered.

He draped an arm along the back of the seat, and the cab, already small, shrank a little more from Sam's perspective.

"I think I've come up with a solution," he said, looking at her intently. "But its success will depend on you."

Sam was finding it more and more difficult to breathe. She caught the neck of her T-shirt and stretched it, craning her head. Was it just her, or was it getting hot inside the cab? Carefully avoiding his knee, Sam leaned to crank the air conditioner up a notch. "How so?"

"Would you agree to let Whiskey stay on here for a while?"

"I already told you that I'd keep him as long as you want, but what good will that do? Colby still won't have her horse."

"No. But if we could pick up the lessons again, it would be a compromise of sorts."

Sam cocked her head over her shoulder to stare at him, her hand stilling on the air conditioner control. "You mean bring Colby here?"

"Yeah. The arrangement would remain the same, except

that Colby and I would come here instead of you driving to the Rivers Ranch.'' He paused to haul in a deep breath. ''That is, if you're willing,'' he added, his uncertainty obvious.

Willing? Sam groaned as she peeled her T-shirt over her head, rehashing her conversation with Nash in her mind. *Obligated* was a much more fitting word. Leaning to the shower stall, she twisted on the faucet, then stepped back and peeled her jeans down her legs. She kicked them into the corner, then stepped beneath the spray and shut the door. Water sluiced over her head, down her back, between her breasts. With a sigh, she turned her face up, letting the spray wash away the day's accumulation of sweat and grime.

How could she say no to Nash when his request was Colby's only chance of spending time with her horse? She couldn't refuse. She knew it, and she suspected that Nash Rivers knew it, too. So now—because she was a softhearted wimp—she'd set herself up for another couple of hours of torture each week with Nash Rivers. Camille would be delighted, Sam was sure.

Frowning, she grabbed the bar of soap from the dish and briskly rubbed it between her hands. She wouldn't think about him, she told herself firmly. Not now. She was hot and tired and deserved to relax after the day she had put in.

The scent of honeysuckle rose, heightened by the steam and friction of her hands. A gift from her sister Merideth, the soap was one of Sam's few concessions to her femininity. Inhaling deeply, she closed her eyes, emptying her mind as she rubbed the fragrant bar down her arms and across her chest. Cupping a breast, she tipped it up, tracing the dark areola, then opened her eyes and dipped her chin, watching the nipple bud.

She closed her palm over her breasts, flattening it, and

let her head drift back as delicious sensations moved through her body in waves. She traced the flow with a sudsy palm, drifting from the swell of her breast, down her abdomen, to the nest of curls between her legs.

Was this how her body would respond to a man's touch? she wondered fleetingly. Would she ever be able to let a man get close enough to find out? Unexpected tears welled up behind her eyes. She wanted so desperately to have what her sister Mandy shared with Jesse, what women all over the world enjoyed every day.

She wanted to experience desire firsthand. She wanted a man to touch her and not know fear. She wanted to feel a man's lips on hers without also feeling repulsion. She wanted to feel the heat of a man's body, the scent of his masculinity and not feel as if she were suffocating. She wanted to laugh and tease and touch without remembering the man who had robbed her of the ability to do all those things.

Closing her eyes, she let her mind go, plucking the memory of Nash's hand at her cheek from those that flashed by. Long, tapered fingers tanned to a rich, golden brown. Gentle, yet strong. Undemanding, yet sure. The hollow of his palm, cupping her jaw. Eyes, hard as flint at moments, yet full of love when turned on his daughter. Teasing at times, full of gut-wrenching emotion at others. A man of many moods, but a man confident in himself and unafraid of displaying his emotions…or of touching.

Sam sighed, dragging her soap-slickened hand back up the length of her body to her breasts. Her fingertips bumped the turgid nipple and electrical shocks ripped through her middle. Would his touch be as gentle here? she wondered dreamily. Would her body respond any differently than when he'd simply touched her cheek?

The tears spilled over her eyelids, mixing with the spray from the shower. Would she ever know? Or was she des-

tined to live her life with her desires locked tightly inside
her own body?

She wanted so desperately to be normal. She wanted so
desperately to be a woman in the fullest sense of the word.
She wanted...with a shuddery sigh, she dropped her chin
to her chest, refusing to give life to that last thought.

She might want Nash Rivers, but he would never want
her. Not in the same way she was beginning to want him.
And why should he? Sam McCloud was an emotional bas-
ket case. A woman, yes, but one who'd worked hard for
years to hide her femininity. And Nash was a man, an un-
believably handsome man, who probably had scores of
beautiful women fighting for his attention.

A woman like Sam wouldn't stand a chance of attracting
a man like Nash Rivers.

"Hey, y'all! Is the lesson over? I've got fresh-squeezed
lemonade for you."

At Mandy's invitation, Sam, Colby and Nash's heads all
turned as if their chins were linked by a single string.

Colby sang out. "Wow! That sounds good!" She squir-
reled down from her horse, tossed Sam the reins and ran
for the fence.

Chuckling, Sam followed, leading Whiskey. Nash fell
into step beside her. "Your family's being awfully nice
about having us here."

Sam lifted a shoulder as she wrapped Whiskey's reins
around the rail, tying him. "It's no hardship."

"All the same, we appreciate the hospitality."

In deference to the suit Nash wore, Sam led the way to
the gate, instead of scaling the fence as Colby had done.
"Six months ago, if you were thirsty, you'd have been
drinking from the trough with the livestock."

He arched a brow in question.

"Mandy used to run the place," Sam explained. "Now
that she's married, she's turned over most of the manage-

ment to Jesse. Gives her more time in the house. She's getting a kick out of doing the little wife-things, like baking and making lemonade. Personally, I hope the newness doesn't wear off any time soon. We used to share the cooking and cleaning chores. Now she does it all.''

When Sam reached for the gate latch, Nash's hand was there first. She whipped her head around to look at him.

''Ladies first,'' he offered, smiling.

Blushing, Sam stepped through then waited while Nash locked the gate behind them.

Turning, he placed a hand at the small of her back, the pressure slight as he headed her toward the truck where Mandy was pouring lemonade from an insulated jug. ''So all of you live together?'' he asked.

Though only two fingers touched her and a layer of cloth separated those two fingers from her skin, Sam felt as if a wall of fire had hit her back. ''Yeah,'' she breathed, focusing on putting one foot in front of the other. ''Mandy and Jesse took the wing where the master bedroom is, so they have their privacy.''

''What privacy?'' Mandy teased, overhearing their conversation. She offered Nash a glass of iced lemonade. ''With our twelve-year-old son underfoot, trying to monopolize his father's attention, there's no such thing as privacy.''

Nash accepted the glass, but couldn't hide his confusion. ''But I thought you were newlyweds?''

Mandy laughed and gave him a pat on the back. ''We are. We just had a little bit of a head start on becoming parents.'' She handed Sam a glass, then winked. ''Sam can tell you the gory details.'' She turned to Colby. ''Would you like to see our new litter of kittens?''

Colby's eyes brightened as she turned to Nash for approval. ''Can I, Daddy, please?''

''Sure, sweetheart.''

Then they were gone and Sam and Nash were alone.

Nash dusted off a spot on the tailgate and sat down. With a glance at Sam, he patted the space beside him, indicating for her to join him. Since there wasn't any other place to sit, Sam grudgingly took the seat offered, but managed to place a good two feet between them.

"So what are the gory details?" he prompted.

Sam propped her glass on the tailgate between them and dug a toe of her boot into the ground. "They aren't gory, really. More like sad. Jesse and Mandy fell in love when they were teenagers, but our dad forbade Mandy to go out with him. You see, there was this ongoing feud between the Barristers and the McClouds, and Daddy couldn't stand the thought of a Barrister marrying one of his daughters.

"Anyway, they started meeting on the sly, and one night Daddy caught them. He put a bullet in Jesse and dragged Mandy home and locked her in her room."

Nash's eyes widened in surprise. "Your father shot Jesse?"

Sam winced, knowing how badly this sounded. "Yeah, but I'd like to believe he only meant to scare him, not hurt him. But whatever his intent, Jesse left town that same night without telling a soul where he was headed. Later, Mandy found out she was pregnant. Of course Jesse didn't know about the baby, and she had no way of locating him to tell him. Nobody heard a word from him until a little over six months ago when he came back to Texas to claim the inheritance Wade Barrister left him."

"And that's when Jesse found out about his son?"

Sam chuckled. "Yeah. I think you can imagine his shock."

"So then they married?"

"Well, no, not right off. They had some things to settle between them first. But it all worked out in the end."

Thoughtfully, Nash took a sip of his lemonade. "What did Jesse's stepmother think of all this?"

"Margo?" Sam sputtered a laugh. "She did all she could

to keep them apart. That old feud worked both ways. The Barristers didn't care for the McClouds any more than the McClouds cared for the Barristers. Margo was determined to own the Circle Bar and she figured if she could turn Jesse against Mandy, he'd leave town again and she could gain control.''

"She's a shrewd businesswoman."

"She's a conniving witch, if you ask me," Sam muttered disagreeably. "She hates Jesse almost as much as she hates the McClouds. She resents the fact that her husband left Jesse the ranch, and she only got the house. She wants the whole kit and caboodle and she'll do anything to get it.

"Personally, I don't understand why she wants it. None of the wranglers on the Circle Bar like her, and would quit if they had to take their orders from her. And she refuses to even acknowledge her neighbors. Considers them beneath her." She cocked her head to peer at him. "How do you know her, anyway?"

"She's one of the investors in the Rivers Ranch development."

Though Nash could tell Sam didn't approve of his association with Margo, she offered no comment. She merely lifted a shoulder. "I guess all money is green, no matter what the source."

Nash set his glass aside and cupped his hands around the rim of the tailgate. He turned his head and looked at Sam. "I appreciate what you're doing for Colby."

Embarrassed, Sam ducked her head and dug her toe a little deeper into the dirt she'd already loosened. "It's nothing."

He leaned closer, his voice softening. "I think Colby would disagree. I know I do." He laid a hand on hers, curling his fingers around hers...and Sam's gaze locked on those fingers, feeling the heat and strength in them. Desperately she tried to focus on what he was saying and not on the heat crawling up her arm.

"I know you won't take money for the lessons. You've already made that clear. But I'd like to do something to show my appreciation. How about dinner? Do you like Italian? There's a great place on Sixth Street in Austin. Sfuzzi's. Have you been there?"

Her eyes still riveted on the hand that covered hers, marveling at the contrast in size, the variation in skin-tone, Sam fought back the panic. Dinner? A date! As much as she'd dreamed of being alone with Nash, she had no experience with dates. "N-no," she stammered. "I've never eaten there."

"Good! How about Friday night?"

"What about Friday night?" Colby asked, skipping up to join them.

Nash and Sam both looked up. Not far behind Colby came Mandy, one arm looped through Jesse's, the other through her son Jaime's. Nash smiled at Colby. "I was just inviting Sam to dinner on Friday night."

A slow grin built on Colby's face as she looked from Nash to Sam, then back again to her dad. "Really? Cool."

Sam tore her hand from beneath Nash's and hopped down from the tailgate. "I didn't say I'd go," she mumbled, stuffing her hands into her pockets.

"Go where?" Mandy asked, joining them.

"Daddy's taking Sam to dinner Friday night," Colby told her.

Mandy raised a brow, looking at Sam, her surprise obvious. "Really?"

"I—"

But before Sam could deny her acceptance of the invitation, Nash was levering himself from the tailgate, interrupting her. "About seven, then," he said, and turned to Colby. "Well, I guess we better get out of here before we wear out our welcome. Let's go unsaddle Whiskey and put him back in his stall."

Sam stood, staring after them, her heart pounding a hole

in her chest. Dinner? Oh, God! How could she have let this happen? Her blood ran cold as another thought formed. What if Nash was like those men she'd read about, who assumed that by buying a woman dinner they were entitled to a roll in her bed? Dreaming about making love with him was one thing, but doing it was something else! She wasn't ready for this! She didn't know if she'd *ever* be ready for this! Oh, Lord, what was she going to do now?

Colby sat on the bathroom counter, watching Nash put the finishing touches on a Windsor knot in his tie. "You look handsome, Daddy."

Nash smiled at his daughter's reflection in the bathroom mirror. "Thanks, sweetheart."

Colby scooted along the counter and reached for the knot, fussing with it. "Are you going to kiss her?"

Nash dropped his chin and stared...then laughed. "This isn't a date, Colby."

"Well, what is it then?"

"It's just—well," he stammered, "it's—it's just a way of showing Sam how much we appreciate her giving you lessons."

Colby bit back a grin. "Uh-huh," she replied, obviously not believing a word he said.

"Colby?"

"In here, Nina," Colby yelled back. She made a face at Nash in the mirror and whispered, "I'll bet you five dollars she says, 'Well, there you are, you little scamp.'"

Nash tossed back his head and laughed at his daughter's impersonation of her grandmother. "You're on."

At that moment, Nina appeared in the doorway, her plump face flushed. "There you are, you little scamp. I've been looking all over for you."

Smiling smugly, Colby stuck out her hand. "Pay up, sucker."

Chuckling, Nash pulled a money clip from his slacks pocket and peeled off a five-dollar bill.

"And what is that for?" Nina demanded to know.

Nash caught Colby under the arms and set her on the floor. "Just paying off a little wager."

Nina frowned at them both. "You shouldn't encourage her. Gambling's a sin, you know." As if just noticing how Nash was dressed, she arched a brow. "Do you have plans tonight?"

"Daddy has a date."

Nina's gaze snapped to Nash, her surprise obvious.

"It's not a date, exactly," he explained.

"It's a date," Colby insisted as she skipped for the door. "I think Daddy's sweet on Sam."

Nina drew herself erect, her displeasure obvious. "I didn't realize you were seeing anyone."

Nash inhaled deeply, feeling the guilt seep in. "I'm not. Since Sam won't accept money for Colby's riding lessons, I'm taking her out to dinner as thanks for all the time she's spending with us."

Whether Nina accepted the explanation or not, Nash wasn't sure, but she stepped toward him, reaching to adjust his tie. "Stacy liked that color on you," she said, giving the soft silk a final pat. "She always claimed it brought out the blue in your eyes."

The reminder of his former wife had the desired effect, for guilt ate its way a little deeper into Nash. He caught Nina's hand in his, gently removing it from his chest. "I remember, Nina," he murmured. "You don't have to remind me."

Four

Sam did something she rarely, if ever, did...she stood in front of her dresser mirror and stared at herself. Of course it was Mandy who had shoved her in front of the mirror. Sam would never willingly seek her own reflection.

Standing behind Sam, Mandy pressed her hands over her lips, blinking back tears. "You look beautiful."

"I look like a streetwalker," Sam grumbled and gave the bodice of the dress a tug upward, trying to shorten the V at the neckline that dipped down between her breasts.

"You don't either," Mandy scolded. She fussed around Sam, fluffing her hair, and the thick brown locks she had insisted on curling fell around Sam's slim shoulders in waves. Late-afternoon sunlight from the window behind them reflected the golden highlights in Sam's brown hair and danced on the delicate strips of silver that dangled from her ears.

To Sam, the woman in the mirror looked like a stranger.

Unexpected tears welled in her eyes. "I can't do this," she muttered dismally, slumping down onto the foot of the bed.

Mandy plucked a tissue from her pocket and pressed it into Sam's hand. "You can and you will. And don't you dare cry. You'll ruin your mascara."

Sam sniffed, swiping the tissue beneath her nose. "You sound like Merideth."

"I wish she were here and could see you right now. She'd be so proud."

"I'm glad she's not. If she were, she'd probably be stuffing my bra with toilet paper."

Mandy laughed. "You're probably right."

The sound of a car driving up had both women turning their heads to the window. At the sight of Nash's Mercedes, a covey of bats burst into flight in Sam's stomach. "Oh, God," she murmured. "He's here."

Seconds later, the doorbell rang, confirming his arrival. Mandy caught Sam's hand, pulling her to her feet. "You'll do fine," she promised, draping an arm around Sam's shoulders as she guided her toward the bedroom door. "Just relax and enjoy yourself."

Sam dug in her heels, slapping her hands against the door frame. "Mandy, I can't do this. Tell him I'm sick or something. Heck, tell him I died!"

Mandy firmed her lips. "I'll do no such thing." She put a determined shoulder against Sam's back and all but shoved her out into the hall. "Now you behave yourself and act like a lady."

"It'll be an act all right," Sam muttered miserably. "There isn't a ladylike bone in my body."

"Hi, Nash." Jesse extended a hand in greeting. "Come on in. Sam should be just about ready."

Nash returned the handshake and stepped across the threshold. "I hope I'm not—" The words "too early" died on his lips as his gaze landed on Sam, who had just made the turn into the entry hall. He had to do a double take to make sure that it was in fact Sam standing there. Hair usually scraped up in a ponytail and covered with a gimme hat now fell in soft curls past her shoulders. And she was wearing a dress! Calf-length, exposing only a short expanse of bare legs, but a dress! And the wheat-colored silk did something to her eyes, panning the gold from those brown depths and making them sparkle.

Nash wasn't sure what he'd expected, but it certainly wasn't this!

He took a step toward her, then stopped, unsure how to approach this "new" Sam. He extended the bouquet of fresh wildflowers. "These are for you," he said. "Colby picked them."

Sam stared at the bouquet as if it was a loaded .45 aimed dead on her chest. No one had ever given her flowers before. Never. And to think that Colby would do such a kind thing for her made a lump rise to her throat.

A nudge from behind her made Sam stumble forward. She shot a dark look over her shoulder at her sister as she accepted the bouquet. "Thanks," she murmured to Nash.

Before her fingers had fully closed around the stems, Mandy was snatching the flowers from Sam's hands. "I'll put these in water for you," she offered helpfully. "I'm sure y'all are anxious to be on your way."

"Well, we do have a seven-thirty reservation," Nash replied gratefully.

Jesse opened the front door again and gave Sam a wink. "Don't stay out too late, you two."

"I'll have her home by midnight, I promise." Taking Sam by the elbow, Nash guided her through the doorway. At his car, he reached for the door handle and bumped Sam's hand as she did the same.

She snatched back her hand.

"Allow me," he said with a bow and opened the door for her.

Her cheeks flaming, Sam slid onto the seat and glanced at her wristwatch. It read 7:03. Oh, God, how would she ever survive until midnight?

"You look lovely tonight, Sam."

Sam slunk lower in her seat, raising the menu to hide her face. The lights were low—thank goodness—which hopefully would help conceal the blotches of red she was sure stained her neck and cheeks. "Thanks," she mumbled.

"I've never seen you in a dress before. You should wear them more often."

"Kind of hard to throw a calf and castrate him while wearing a dress," she replied dryly.

Nash chuckled. "I imagine that's true." He reached across the table, curling a finger over the top of her menu and tipping it down. Her startled gaze met his over candlelight. "Are you going to hide behind that thing all night?"

"I'm trying to decide what to order."

"How about if I order for both of us?"

Reluctantly, Sam laid aside the menu. Since she didn't recognize anything listed, letting him choose was probably best. "All right."

A waiter appeared. "May I offer you something from the bar?" he asked politely.

Nash glanced at Sam. "Their Bellini is excellent."

Though she hadn't a clue what a Bellini was, Sam figured that since it was coming from the bar it was bound to have alcohol in it and she could use a good stiff drink right then. "A Bellini's fine."

Nash ordered two, then turned his gaze back on Sam...and smiled.

That smile was almost Sam's undoing. Heavens, but he was handsome! And when he smiled, there was a little dimple on his left cheek that deepened. And that mouth! Merideth would call it kissable, but in Sam's estimation, kissable didn't come close to describing those delectable lips.

The lower one was a little fuller than the upper and the upper lip almost disappeared as his smile broadened, revealing rows of even white teeth.

She tried her best to return his smile, but her own lips felt as if they were set in cement. Her shoulders sagged in defeat. "Look," she said miserably. "We don't have to do this."

Nash looked at her, his smile drifting down into a puzzled frown. "Do what?"

Sam gestured toward the table. "This dinner thing."

"Aren't you hungry?"

"No. In fact, I feel like I'm going to throw up."

Nash choked back a laugh at her bluntness. "I take it you regret accepting my invitation."

"I'm not sure that I ever did," she muttered. "Not that I don't appreciate what you're trying to do," she hastened to add. "But it isn't necessary. I like Colby. And I sure as heck don't expect any compensation for giving her a few riding lessons."

Nash smiled again. A loose kind of easy smile this time that had Sam's tense shoulders relaxing the teeniest bit. "Colby likes you, too. In fact, I'm afraid her feelings for you border on hero worship."

Sam blushed, but did manage a smile in return. "I'm no hero. I just understand her love for her horse."

The waiter arrived and placed a drink in front of each of them. With a nod of thanks to the waiter, Nash lifted his glass in a toast. "To Sam, the rescuer of doomed horses and the mender of little girls' broken hearts."

Rolling her eyes, Sam took a sip of her drink. "You give me way too much credit."

"Maybe not enough." He rested his arms on the table, studying her, still in shock over the change in her appearance. "You're a fascinating bundle of contradictions. Tell me about yourself."

Self-consciously, Sam smoothed a finger down the side

of her glass, gathering condensation on the tip of her finger. "There isn't much to tell."

"I think there is. For starters, why don't you tell me why you chose to become a veterinarian?"

Sam touched the drop of condensation to her tongue, totally unaware of the sensuality behind the gesture...or its effect on Nash. "I grew up on a ranch surrounded by animals. When I was little, I used to trail Gabe, our foreman, and watch him doctor the livestock. Before long, I was doctoring them myself."

The tip of that pink tongue darted out again, licking the last droplet of water from her finger...and Nash felt his groin tighten in response. Surprised by his reaction to her, he forced his attention back to the conversation. "Did your father encourage this interest?"

"My dad?" Sam snorted indelicately. "Hardly. In fact, if he'd lived, I'd never have become a vet." Noting his surprise, Sam explained. "Daddy wouldn't let any of us go away to college. Flat-out refused. Said all the education we needed he could provide right there on the Double-Cross. We went round and round with him over it. Especially Merideth. She wanted to go to acting school in New York. But he wouldn't budge. Once he made his mind up about something, there was no changing it."

"Sounds like a stubborn man."

"Oh, he was stubborn all right. And he always got his way."

Nash looked at her across the table. Candlelight flickered on high cheekbones, highlighted full lips moistened from the peach-flavored drink, and teased at the shadows between her breasts exposed by the generous V in her blouse. As he stared, he wondered if she realized how beautiful she was, how sexy, and wondered further why he'd never noticed it before now. But he knew better than to comment on it. He'd already learned that compliments made her uneasy. "Do you enjoy your work?" he asked instead.

"I love it, though my business is small."

"Where's your clinic located?"

Sam chuckled, circling a finger around the rim of her glass. "In my truck."

He arched a brow in surprise.

"I've never wanted the kind of restrictions a clinic demands, though I have commandeered a room in the barn for my supplies. I limit my practice to ranch and farm calls. If X-rays or surgery are required, I refer my clients to one of the other practices nearby."

"Wouldn't it be more profitable to set up your own clinic so that you could offer a full line of services?"

"Probably."

"Then why not do it?"

She lifted a shoulder and took a sip of her drink. "Being cramped up inside all day doesn't appeal to me." She set her drink down, and folded her forearms along the table. "What about you?" she said, redirecting the conversation his way. "Colby tells me you inherited Rivers Ranch from your father."

He shuddered visibly. "I hate to think what all she had to say on *that* subject."

Sam laughed, the first real laugh Nash had ever heard from her. The sound was full, yet feminine, and made his own smile widen.

"Don't worry," Sam assured him. "She didn't reveal any deep, dark family secrets, although I did get the impression that she wished you were a rancher and not a developer."

"I'm afraid my choice of career is a huge disappointment to my daughter."

"I wouldn't go so far as to say that, but I do know that the idea of leaving Rivers Ranch saddens her. She seems to love it there."

Nash smiled ruefully. "She always has. But then that's probably because her experiences there are more like vacations. She doesn't know how difficult life can be on a working ranch.''

''And you do?'' The words were out of her mouth before Sam realized she'd even voiced them. ''Sorry,'' she said, blushing. ''I didn't mean that the way it sounded.''

''No apology necessary. And, yes, I know how hard ranch life is. I grew up on Rivers Ranch.''

Sam leaned forward, unable to hide her surprise. ''Really? I took you for a city slicker. No offense,'' she added hastily. ''But considering the way you are and all, I have a hard time picturing you working on a ranch.''

Biting back a smile, Nash leaned forward too. ''Believe it or not, I can rope and brand with the best of them. I just choose not to.''

Sam sank back into her chair. ''Wow,'' she murmured. ''Who'd have ever thought?'' She stared at him, trying to imagine him covered in grime, holding a steer down in the dirt while pressing a hot branding iron to its hide. The image simply wouldn't form. ''Then why don't you?'' she blurted out. She leaned forward again, her expression earnest. ''I mean, why don't you put the ranch back into operation instead of cutting it all up and selling off the pieces? It wouldn't take much, I'd bet. The pastures need cleaning, but the soil is good. You'd need to do some work on the barn, but, heck, you could hire someone to do that. And since cattle prices are down right now, it would be the perfect time to—''

Nash threw up a hand to stop her. ''No way. I've had a stomach full of ranch life.''

''But—''

''I know you mean well,'' he said, interrupting her. ''But nothing you say will convince me to go back to ranching. I watched my grandfather and my father sweat blood over that place, sacrificing everything, including their health, to keep from losing the land when times were rough. As far as my father was concerned, he didn't have a family, he had the land, and that's all he ever wanted.''

Sam heard the bitterness in his voice. "And you resent him for that," she said knowingly.

"Whether I resent him or not doesn't matter anymore. My father's gone and soon the ranch will be, too. Besides, I like what I do and I'm good at it. I can sleep at night, not worrying about the weather or the price of grain or the price of beef on the hoof." Realizing how worked up he was getting, he smiled ruefully. "Sorry. As you can probably tell, Rivers Ranch is a sore spot with me." He forced himself to settle back in his chair, anxious to change the subject. "Now why don't you tell me about this other sister of yours. Merideth, isn't it?"

Sam lay in her bed staring at the ceiling, sleep the last thing on her mind. Adrenaline pumped through her veins, keeping her eyes wide open, her mind clicking like a computer sorting data.

She'd done it. She'd actually gone out with a man and survived. Not only survived, she thought with a small measure of pride, but enjoyed herself immensely.

Of course, the credit was due to Nash. He was a gentleman through and through, and so easy to talk to that she'd forgotten her nervousness...at least for a while. There had been that moment of awkwardness when he'd walked her to the door. He'd taken her hand, and for a minute she'd thought that he meant to kiss her.

But he hadn't. He'd simply squeezed her hand, then released it and thanked her for an enjoyable evening.

Sam pressed two fingers to her lips, wondering what it would have been like if he'd actually kissed her. Would she have panicked? Would she have been repulsed? Would she have melted at his feet?

Grabbing the covers, she pulled them over her head,

groaning. "Grow up, Sam," she told herself firmly. It was a date. Nothing more.

But she still had her dreams.

While Sam was pulling the covers over her head, Nash was tiptoeing down the hall of his own house, hoping to make it to his room without being detected.

"Nash? Is that you?"

He halted, grimacing as a light snapped on in his mother-in-law's room. Feeling like a teenager caught sneaking in after curfew, he took a few steps backwards and stuck his head into her room.

"Yes, ma'am, it's me."

She pulled on glasses, peering at the clock beside her bed. "Goodness! It's after one!" she exclaimed, looking up at him in surprise.

But Nash refused to feel guilty. Hell! He'd taken a woman to dinner. Where was the crime in that?

"Did Colby give you any problems?" he asked, hoping to divert her attention from the lateness of the hour.

Her expression softened. "She was an angel. We decided against watching *The Little Mermaid* again, opting instead to look through old scrapbooks." She sighed dramatically and pulled a handkerchief from the cuff of her nightgown's sleeve to dab at an eye. Nash knew she was setting him up for something, but what? He didn't have to wait long to find out.

"It was difficult for me, of course," she went on, "but Colby so loves looking at pictures of her mother. Your and Stacy's wedding album is her favorite." She pressed her handkerchief against trembling lips, then turned her watery gaze on Nash. "Sometimes it's so hard to believe that she's gone. It's seems like only yesterday that the two of you married. I miss her so much."

The reminder was well-aimed and ripped through Nash's heart with the brutality of a serrated knife. "Yes, Nina," he said, wearily, "I miss her, too." He backed from the door. "If you'll excuse me, I think I'll head on to bed. It's been a long day."

Hands, clever competent hands that teased and seduced moved over his shoulders, his back, kneading the muscles in his arms, splaying over his chest and abdomen, flicking a nail against his aroused nipples. Lips full and luscious drew on his own, sucking him deeper and deeper into the web of desire that weaved itself around them. Beneath him she moved, her skin as sleek as satin where it rubbed against his, her slender hips arching high to meet his.

He could feel the heat building within him. His manhood straining to meet her, to join with her, to mate with her. To make them one. He knotted his hands in the tangle of long brown hair haloing her face on his pillow.

"Sam," he murmured, nearly drunk with the taste of her. "Oh, Sam," he cried as he entered her and her velvet flesh closed around him. The heat built, nearly blinding him, as sensation after sensation stacked one upon the other, filling him to near bursting. "Now," he groaned. "I want you now."

Nash awakened abruptly, pushing himself to his elbows, his body drenched in sweat. His chest rose and fell in deep, grabbing gulps for air as he looked around his bedroom and found himself alone. A dream, he told himself. Just a dream. He twisted, his legs tangling in the sheet as he groped blindly for the lamp beside his bed.

He found the knob and light flooded the room. He closed his eyes, blocking out the shocking brightness, then opened them…and found himself staring at a picture of Stacy.

"Oh, God," he groaned, falling back against his pillows. He pressed his fists against his eyes. How had this happened? he asked himself in growing panic. How had he allowed himself to become physically attracted to Sam? When he'd lost Stacy, he'd sworn that he'd never become involved with another woman. For almost seven long years, he'd held to that pledge.

Dropping his fists from his eyes, he leaned over, plucking the picture from his nightstand. He settled back against his pillows and propped the frame on his abdomen. Stacy. His wife. The woman he'd promised to love and cherish until death do us part. He waited for the guilt to seep in. The sense of betrayal for thinking intimate thoughts of another woman.

Nothing surfaced but the familiar anger.

He sighed, closing his eyes and pressing his head back against the pillows. Stacy had lied to him. She'd deceived him. And in the end he'd lost her. Anger tightened his chest, firmed his lips. The doctors had told her not to get pregnant. They'd warned her of the dangers. A woman who was already suffering kidney problems from advancing diabetes would never survive a pregnancy.

But Stacy, stubborn Stacy, had ignored their warnings. She'd only pretended to take the birth-control pills her doctor had prescribed. She'd gotten pregnant, and then hidden her pregnancy from Nash until she was over three months along.

He remembered well the day she had told him about the baby they'd created together. At first, he'd been too shocked to respond, then he'd become angry, shouting at her, demanding that she terminate the pregnancy. Finally, he'd been reduced to begging.

But she'd refused.

Stubborn Stacy. Determined to have the baby she longed for, convinced that she was strong enough to survive the demands the baby would make on her body.

But she hadn't survived, though she had lived longer than the doctors had predicted. She'd lived eight hours after giving birth to Colby. Long enough to hold the baby she'd gambled her life on, long enough to name her daughter…but not long enough to erase Nash's anger with her.

And that was where the guilt lay with Nash. He'd accepted his wife's death, healed the wounds her passing had left on his heart, but he'd never gotten over his anger with her for robbing him of whatever life they might have had together. And because he couldn't let go of his anger, he felt a tremendous guilt. Nina only increased that guilt by trying so desperately to keep her daughter's memory alive.

Nash sighed, replacing the picture on his nightstand. He touched the pad of a finger to Stacy's cheek. He didn't need Nina's constant reminders. He remembered Stacy. He always would. But she was gone. That had been her choice and there was nothing he could do to bring her back.

But there was something he could do about this attraction he was beginning to feel for Sam. He wouldn't get involved with her. It wouldn't be fair. Not when he was still burdened with this guilt, this anger with Stacy.

"Daddy said he had a good time Friday night."

Sam kicked over a barrel and sent it rolling. "He did, huh?"

Colby trailed Sam, leading Whiskey. "Yeah, and he said you looked absolutely gorgeous."

Shocked, Sam whirled to stare.

Colby squenched up her nose and giggled. "I think he likes you."

Sam glanced at the Mercedes parked by the arena and at Nash, who sat inside talking on a cellular phone. She forced herself to stoop and pull the barrel upright. "You shouldn't say things like that, Colby."

"Why not? It's true." She fell into step behind Sam again, as they headed for the next barrel. "Did he kiss you good-night?"

Sam jerked to a stop and whirled. "Colby!"

Unfazed, the girl peered up at Sam, her look an odd combination of impertinence and innocence. "Well, did he?"

Sam turned away, marching toward the next barrel. "That's none of your business."

"When Daddy says that, it usually means yes."

"Well, when *I* say it, it means just that. It's none of your business."

"I'll bet he did kiss you," Colby said smugly, "because your face is so red. Are you going out with him again?"

"No."

"Did he ask you?"

"No."

"He will."

Exasperated, Sam turned. "Are you going to ride that horse or lead him around all day?"

Colby grinned, showing off that missing front tooth. "I'm gonna ride. Will you give me a boost up?"

Frowning, Sam cupped her hands and Colby stuck a boot in the cradle she'd made. With a heave upwards, Sam settled her in the saddle. "Warm him up," she instructed, and turned away.

"Sam?" Colby called out, stopping her.

"What?"

"I think you're pretty, too."

Though she wanted to hold on to her anger with the child, Sam discovered she couldn't. Chuckling, she shook her head. The kid was too dang much. "Thanks, Colby."

Sam stole a glance over her shoulder in the direction of Nash's car. He still sat behind the wheel with his cellular phone propped between shoulder and ear. He had a notebook of some kind braced against the steering wheel and was writing furiously as he talked. The fact that he hadn't ventured from the car since his arrival with Colby almost an hour earlier began to eat at Sam.

She didn't know what she'd expected from him, but some kind of acknowledgement of the evening they'd spent together would have gone a long way in negating her own doubts about its success. Even a casual "Hi, how are you doing?" would have beaten this awkward silence.

With a sigh, she turned her gaze back to the center of the arena where Colby was practicing figure eights. Colby was wrong, Sam told herself. Nash hadn't had a good time. In fact, he was probably sitting out the lesson in his car in order to avoid having to talk to her again.

Two quick blasts from the Mercedes's horn had Sam turning again in his direction. As she watched, the window glided down and Nash stuck out his head. "Time's up, Colby!" he yelled. "Let's go."

"Oh, Daddy," she whined. "Just a little bit longer?"

"No, and no arguments." His head disappeared inside the car again and the window slid back up. He never once glanced Sam's way.

"I went to dinner with him last Friday night."

Camille arched a brow. "Oh? And how was it?"

Sam slumped in the chair, scrunching her mouth to one side. "Miserable."

"For you or for him?"

Sam wanted to lie and say for both of them, but an innate honesty made her reply, "Him."

"Did he tell you that?"

"Not in so many words."

"Then how do you know he was miserable?"

Sam lifted a shoulder. "It was obvious."

"Was he rude?"

"No. He was a perfect gentleman."

"Then what was it about his behavior that made you think he was miserable?"

"Nothing that night. It was yesterday, at Colby's lesson, that I realized the night was a flop."

"And what happened at the lesson to make you think this?"

"He sat in his car and talked on his cellular phone the entire time."

"So you *assumed* he didn't enjoy your evening together."

"It doesn't take a rocket scientist to figure that one out," Sam replied dryly.

"Isn't it possible that he had pressing business matters to attend to?"

"It's possible, but I doubt it. At all her other lessons, Nash has insisted on being in the arena with us."

Thoughtfully, Camille ran her pen through graceful fingers, then laid it aside. "Let's forget about yesterday's lesson for a moment and focus on your impressions of the evening. Let's begin with you telling me where he took you."

"Sfuzzi's."

Camille nodded approvingly. "A lovely restaurant with lots of atmosphere and excellent cuisine."

"I wouldn't know." At Camille's puzzled look, Sam added, "I barely ate anything."

"Why?"

Sam squirmed uncomfortably in her chair. "I don't know. Too nervous, I guess."

"Does he make you feel uncomfortable?"

"That's putting it mildly."

"Explain for me, please."

Sam sighed, propping her elbows on the chair's arms and lacing her fingers across her abdomen. "First, he's a man and all men make me nervous."

Camille held up a hand, stopping Sam before she could go on. "Not *all* men make you nervous. You have a very nice relationship with your brother-in-law."

"Yeah, but that's different. Jesse's family."

"He wasn't always. I distinctly remember meeting with you shortly after he returned. As I recall, he received an injury to his arm that you considered your fault and you administered first aid.''

Sam remembered the incident, too, and how difficult it had been for her to touch Jesse, but for the life of her she couldn't figure out where Camille was going with this. ''So?''

''You were afraid of him, but you overcame that fear once you realized that he meant you no harm.''

Sam narrowed an eye. ''And you think that once I realize Nash doesn't mean to harm me, I'll be able to relax around him, too?''

''It's a possibility worth considering.''

Sam tossed back her head and laughed at the ceiling. ''You've got to be kidding! The guy ties me in knots!''

''But you're attracted to him.''

Heat stained Sam's cheeks as the truth burned its way through her. ''Yeah, so what?''

''That attraction may be what is tying you up in knots, not the fact that he is a man.''

Sam slowly sat up straighter in her chair. ''Do you think so?''

''I do.''

Sam's brow furrowed as she gave the possibility consideration. She cocked her head and frowned at Camille. ''Assuming that's true, then what?''

Camille lifted her hands, palms up. ''That's up to you. And Nash of course,'' she added judiciously. ''When will you see him again?''

''My next lesson with Colby is scheduled for Monday.''

''Excellent,'' Camille said, rising. ''And this time, don't wait for him to approach you. *You* make the first move.''

After sending Colby to the barn to unsaddle Whiskey, Sam glanced toward Nash's Mercedes. Just like the last lesson, he'd remained inside his car throughout the entire hour. Kind of hard to make the first move when he was holed up in his luxury bunker on wheels. But Sam was determined to follow Camille's instructions. She strode in the direction of the car and tapped on the window.

Engrossed in a computer printout, Nash jumped at the unexpected intrusion, then quickly pressed the button to lower the window. "What's wrong?" he asked, straining to look behind her. "Where's Colby?"

"Nothing's wrong. She's unsaddling Whiskey." Sam dipped her chin, working up the courage to say aloud the one sentence she'd been practicing for days. She hauled in a steadying breath and lifted her head, meeting his gaze squarely. "I just wanted to thank you again for dinner last week."

When she saw the frown lines that gathered between his eyes, Sam immediately regretted having brought the subject up. "Anyway," she said, her cheeks burning, "I had a good time and just wanted you to know." She took a step back, stuffing her hands into her pockets. "I'll get Colby."

Nash swore under his breath as she whirled away. He'd hurt her, embarrassed her, and Sam didn't deserve that kind of treatment. She was kind and generous to a fault. The least he could give her in return was honesty. And his friendship. There was no harm in that. He stuck his head out the window and shouted, "Sam!"

She slowly turned back to look at him.

He shouldered open the door and stood, bracing an arm along its top. "I had a good time, too."

"You did?"

"Yes, I did. To be honest, the evening turned out much better than I expected."

The reluctance with which he made the admission registered, but the sincerity was there, too, and it was the sincerity that Sam focused on. A warmth spread through her, curving her lips. "For me, too," she said, and took a hesitant step toward him.

Gray eyes held her, and Sam stopped, mesmerized by

the intensity in them. Suddenly self-conscious, she fished in her back pocket for the paper she had tucked there earlier. "I picked this up the other day and thought you might want to give it some consideration."

Nash stretched out a hand and took the wrinkled paper. "What is it?" he asked, shaking it open.

"An entry form for a quarter-horse show in Austin. They have classes in all age groups."

He snapped up his head to look at her. "And you want Colby to compete?"

"She's ready. Plus it will give her the opportunity to meet some other kids who share her interest in horses."

"I don't know," he murmured uncertainly. "Do you really think she's ready for this?"

"I wouldn't suggest it if I didn't. But I would like to get in an extra practice next week if we can."

"When?"

"Wednesday afternoon would work for me."

He shook his head. "I've got meetings all day."

"How about if I just pick her up and bring her over here? You could drop by for her on your way home from work."

"That's a lot to ask of you."

"Not really. I'll be in your area anyway, vaccinating some horses. It wouldn't be any trouble to swing by and pick up Colby."

"If you're sure..."

"I am. Just tell her to be ready around three." Sam started to turn away, then whirled back. "Oh, and Nash," she said, "I'm glad you had a good time, too."

She turned and strode for the barn, her face burning. "Okay, Camille," she muttered under her breath. "I did it. Now what?"

Sam was working in her supply room early Friday morning, unloading a new shipment of supplies, when she heard a car stop in front of the barn. Wiping her hands on a rag, she walked to the barn's entrance. Her heart did a slow flip when she saw that it was Nash.

"Hi," she said, as he stepped from his car. "What are you doing here so early? Our lesson's not until five."

He closed the door and walked toward her. "Yeah, I know, but I thought I'd stop by on my way to the office and let you know that we won't be coming for our lesson today."

Sam frowned and tucked the rag into her back pocket, trying to mask her disappointment. "Oh? Why not?"

"Colby's grounded."

She bit back a smile. "What did she do this time?"

Nash heaved a sigh. "She ripped up all the stakes that the road crew put in place earlier this week."

Sam started to laugh, but quickly sobered when Nash shot her a dark look.

"It's not funny," he grumped. "Now I'll have to order the crew back out to redo the survey. It'll put us weeks behind in cutting the roads."

"Did you ask her why she did it?"

Nash snorted. "Didn't need to. She's made her position clear. She doesn't want to leave Rivers Ranch, so she's doing everything within her power to postpone the inevitable."

That Colby would go to such lengths to stay on the ranch, knowing that she would surely be punished, tugged at Sam's heart. "Do you have to move?" she asked hesitantly. "Couldn't you just build your subdivision somewhere else?"

Nash snapped his head around to frown at her. "You can't just *move* a subdivision. The plans are all laid out to fit that tract of land."

"Would it cost so much to have the plans redrawn? I mean, you have to live somewhere. Why not Rivers Ranch?"

Nash folded his arms across his chest and turned away.

"The cost is irrelevant. I've already told you that I'm not a rancher. I'm a developer. That land means nothing to me but as a potential investment."

"But, Nash—" Sam began.

He turned his wrist, glancing at his watch. "I've got to go. Are you still willing to pick Colby up on Wednesday?"

Sam's shoulders drooped in defeat. The man was just too dang stubborn. "Yeah. Tell her to be ready at three."

"Come on in!"

At Colby's invitation, Sam opened the back door and stepped inside the Rivers' kitchen. Colby sat on a bar stool, tongue tucked determinedly in her cheek as she spread creamy icing over a chocolate cake. An older woman, who Sam assumed was Colby's grandmother, stood at her side, holding the bowl for her. The woman glanced up, her gaze meeting Sam's. Sam saw the disapproval before the woman masked it behind a forced smile.

"Oh, dear! Is it three already?" she asked, setting aside the bowl. She took the knife from Colby's hands. "Run and wash up, sweetie. We don't want to keep your teacher waiting."

Colby shot Sam a grin as she slid off the stool. "Back in a flash," she promised as she skipped from the room.

Sam took another step inside the kitchen, extending her hand. "I don't believe we've met. I'm Sam McCloud."

The woman dropped the knife into the bowl and wiped her hands on her apron before accepting Sam's. "Nancy Bigelow, but everyone calls me Nina."

"It's nice to meet you, Nina. I've heard quite a bit about you from Colby."

Nina chuckled and picked up a pastry bag filled with pink icing. "Yes, our little Colby is quite a talker. She comes by it honestly, though. Her mother—my daughter, Stacy—was a talker, too. Such a friendly person. Never met a stranger." She bent over the cake and began to write.

Intrigued, Sam watched the words *Happy Birthday* take shape.

"You're really good at that," Sam commented, wondering whose birthday was being celebrated. She knew it wasn't Colby's, because Colby had already told her that her birthday was May first, which had passed several months before. Nash's, then?

Nina squeezed off the *y* in Birthday with a flourish. "Years of practice," she replied and leaned over the cake again.

Fascinated by the artistic flair with which the woman manipulated the bag, Sam watched as a pink *S* appeared. A *t* followed and Sam's stomach did a slow flip. *No, it can't be!* she told herself. But before she could deny what her eyes were seeing, an *a* appeared, followed by *c* and *y*. *Happy Birthday Stacy.* Sam silently read the words and glanced up to find Nina watching her.

"Today is Stacy's birthday," Nina said cheerfully. "We're having a special dinner tonight to celebrate. All of Stacy's favorite foods. Chicken-fried steak, mashed potatoes, English peas. And, of course, chocolate cake."

Sam was struck dumb. She didn't have a clue how to respond. A birthday party for a dead woman? She'd never heard of such a thing! Thankfully, she was saved from having to come up with a response by Colby's appearance.

"Are you ready to go?" Colby asked, dancing up to Sam's side.

"Yeah," Sam replied, tearing her gaze from the decorated cake. "Let's get out of here."

Five

Sam was a wreck throughout the riding lesson, worrying about whether or not she should mention the birthday cake to Nash when he came to pick up Colby. In her mind, such fascination with a dead person was unhealthy. Spooky, even. She wasn't sure if Nash was aware of Nina's plans, but she *was* worried about the emotional effect all this might have on Colby.

A shiver chased down her spine as she pictured again that birthday cake, and she forced her attention to Colby, who was putting Whiskey through a maze of cones, practicing lateral moves. "That's it for the day, Colby," she called out. "Walk him a few laps to cool him down."

"Looks like I'm just in time."

Sam turned to find Nash standing behind her. She'd been so caught up in her thoughts that she hadn't heard him arrive. Though it was obvious he'd come straight from work, he'd loosened his tie and removed his jacket. Mandy stood at his side.

"Are y'all done for the day?" her sister asked.

"Yeah."

"Good! We're cooking hamburgers out on the grill and I thought Colby and Nash might like to join us."

Colby rode by at that moment and heard the invitation. "Can we, Daddy? Please?" she begged as she guided Whiskey up to the fence.

By the amiable smile on his face, Sam knew Nash was going to accept the invitation, but before he could, she stepped between him and his daughter, blocking Colby from his vision. "Could I talk to you for a minute?" she asked. At his puzzled look, she added, "In private."

He lifted a shoulder, peering at her curiously. "Well, sure."

Sam climbed the fence and dropped to the other side, then headed for a shade tree on the far side of the barn. Nash fell into step beside her. As soon as they were out of range of Mandy and Colby's hearing, she stopped and turned to him. "You and Colby can't eat with us."

Nash stared at her, his surprise obvious. "All right," he said slowly.

"What I mean is," Sam said in frustration, "is that Nina has planned a special dinner for y'all tonight."

Nash's face relaxed into a smile of relief. "Oh, if that's the only problem, I'll call her. She'll understand."

Sam caught her lower lip between her teeth. "I don't think so." At Nash's puzzled look, Sam heaved a sigh. "She's planning a birthday party for Stacy," she blurted out. "She's baked a cake and everything."

The blood drained from his face. "Oh, dear God," he murmured. Just as quickly, the blood raced back, flushing his cheeks a livid red. His lips thinned to a thin white line of fury. He whirled, turning his back on Sam and paced away a few steps. "I should've known she'd pull something like this," he muttered angrily.

"Like what?" Sam asked, confused.

Nash spun, tossing a hand up in the air. "Like this! She's constantly shoving reminders of Stacy at Colby and me, but she's never gone this far. I suppose it's because of you."

"Me?" Sam asked incredulously. "What do I have to do with any of this?"

"Colby's crazy about you and she's convinced that you and I are—well—" he stammered, suddenly embarrassed "—well, that we're involved or something."

Sam's breath came out in a rush. "Involved? You mean, like—"

Nash frowned, nodding. "Yeah, like that."

Sam placed a hand at her throat, suddenly feeling faint. "But we're not."

"Yeah," he agreed dryly. "But try convincing Colby of that." He stuffed his hands in his pockets. "Listen, Sam, I'm sorry to have involved you in all this."

Sam swallowed hard. "You don't owe me an apology. It's Colby you should be worried about." She shuddered remembering that birthday cake, and the cheerfulness with which Nina had set about decorating it. "It just doesn't seem natural to celebrate the birthday of someone who... well, who's dead," she finally said, unable to think of a gentler way to express it. "I worry about the emotional impact on Colby."

"You're right. It isn't natural, and I intend to put a stop to it before it goes any further." He set his jaw and turned his face to the sky, already dreading the confrontation. After a moment, he lowered his gaze to meet Sam's again. "I hate to impose on you like this, but could I leave Colby here? I don't want her around when I discuss this with Nina."

"Well, yeah, sure."

"I don't know how long I'll be gone..." he began uncertainly.

"Don't worry about Colby," she assured him. "She'll be fine."

Colby, exhausted after roughhousing with Jaime and the dogs, had crashed around nine. It was almost ten now, and Sam was beginning to worry. Was it possible that Nina had turned on Nash, harming him in some way? Sam squeezed her palms against her temples, squelching the thought. No, she told herself firmly. The woman might be a little off, but she wasn't dangerous. Pathetic, maybe. But not dangerous. She was simply a mother who had loved her daughter dearly and was having a hard time accepting her death.

Unable to stand the waiting any longer, Sam opened the front door, seeking the porch and a clearer view of the drive. She dropped down on the steps to watch for Nash's return.

Moonlight filtered through the trees surrounding the McCloud homestead, tatting the thick saint augustine grass on the front lawn into a lacy web of silver and dark green. A breeze wafted across the wide porch, bringing with it the scent of honeysuckle, Sam's favorite fragrance. She inhaled deeply, closing her eyes, letting her shoulders relax muscle by muscle. When she opened them again, twin points of light danced on the drive.

She bolted to her feet, watching as Nash's car approached. He parked in front of the house and climbed wearily from his car. Moonlight played over his features and Sam's heart twisted at the exhaustion she saw etched there, in the dejected slump of his shoulders.

"Oh, Nash," she said sympathetically. She wanted to hold him, to comfort him, but the best she could do was to lay a hand on his arm.

Before she knew what was happening, he was drawing her closer, wrapping his arms loosely at her waist. He pulled her to him and rested his cheek against the top of her head.

A sigh shuddered through him, reverberating through Sam and drawing a lump to her throat. Forgetting her own fears, she tightened her arms around him and offered him the only thing she was physically capable of giving...her comfort.

And comfort was exactly what Nash needed. He was drained, both emotionally and physically after the confrontation with Nina. The hours spent trying to reason with her had been difficult and exhausting. But the warmth of Sam's body slowly seeped into his, chasing away the chill of loneliness, melting away the layers of guilt and frustration.

He drew Sam closer, burying his nose in her hair. He desperately needed to forget Nina's hysterics, the accusations she'd hurled his way. Inhaling deeply, he filled his senses with the scent of honeysuckle that filled the night air but seemed to begin and end with Sam. Gradually he became aware of the soft curves pressed against him, the swell of breasts, the tautness of the abdomen that nestled so perfectly against his groin, the feel of gentle fingers soothing the tension from his back.

Stepping back, he drew his hands to her elbows, and their gazes met in the moonlight and he nearly lost himself in the depths of brown eyes brimming with compassion. Her hair draped one shoulder and blew in wisps across her cheek. He caught the stray locks and tucked them behind her ear. In the moonlight, he could see the stain of pink on her cheeks, feel the tremble of nerves beneath her skin.

"Are you okay?" she whispered softly.

"Yeah," he said on a sigh. "At least, now I am. Thank you."

"Was it bad?" she asked hesitantly.

Sighing again, he shifted, keeping a hand on one of her elbows as he guided her back to the porch. "Let's just say it wasn't anything I want to repeat anytime soon. Where's Colby?"

"Asleep. For about an hour," she added. He looked so

miserable and so exhausted, Sam wanted desperately to do something for him. "Have you eaten? Can I get you anything?"

"A beer sure would taste good right now."

"I'll get you one. Wait here." Sam disappeared into the house and returned moments later. Nash sat on the steps and Sam sank down beside him, passing him the cold bottle.

"Thanks," he murmured before tipping it up and taking a long swig. He sighed and set the beer aside. "I don't think I've ever done anything harder in my life," he said miserably.

Unable to resist, Sam closed her hand over his and squeezed. "Oh, Nash, I'm so sorry."

He squinted up at the moon. "Yeah, me, too."

Sam saw the glimmer of tears in his eyes and had to swallow back the lump of emotion that rose in her throat. "What did you say to her?"

"Basically, I just told her that there wouldn't be a birthday party tonight, or any other night."

"How did she accept the news?"

"Not well. She cried." He shook his head and turned his hand over to lace his fingers with Sam's. The gesture was an unconscious one, but he clung to her like a drowning man would a lifeline. "She blamed me. Told me that it was my fault that Stacy had died. Said that if I hadn't gotten her pregnant, then she'd be alive today."

"Oh, Nash," Sam murmured. "That's not fair."

"Fair or not, it's the truth." His fingers tightened on hers. He stared out into the darkness, his face a mask of raw pain. "I was the one who planted the seed. It's only natural that Nina would blame me."

"But you couldn't have known that she'd die having the baby," Sam argued.

"But I did know." He sighed, his shoulders drooping under the weight of the guilt Nina had heaped on him.

"The doctors had warned us from the beginning that Stacy shouldn't have children. But she wouldn't listen. She was determined to have a baby. So she quit taking her birth-control pills."

"Did you know she was doing this?"

"No. Not until it was too late. I begged her to have an abortion. Because of her diabetes, the doctors would have performed one. But she refused."

"Nash, it isn't your fault," Sam told him firmly. "Stacy made the decision, not you."

"Yeah, but try telling Nina that."

Sam didn't have a reply. She'd met Nina, seen the depth of her love for her daughter. It would be easier for her to place the blame of Stacy's death on someone, anyone, rather than where it belonged...with her daughter.

Nash's shoulder moved against hers in a sigh. "I'm sorry. I shouldn't be involving you in this."

"You have nothing to apologize for. I involved myself when I told you about the party Nina had planned."

"Yes, but—"

She squeezed his hand, silencing him. "Colby is the most important person here. We have to concern ourselves with her best interests."

Nash stared at her as if seeing her for the first time. He'd never met a woman so unselfish, so compassionate. "You are one hell of a woman," he murmured.

Sam swallowed hard, dropping her gaze. "No, I'm—"

He tucked a knuckle beneath her chin and forced her face back to his. Friendship? Is that what he had told himself he would give her? No harm in that, he remembered thinking. But at the moment, friendship was the last thing on his mind. "You *are* one hell of a woman," he repeated softly.

He was going to kiss her. Sam could see the intent in his eyes, in the way his tongue moved slowly around his lips to moisten them, in the increased pressure of his fingers on her hand. Could she do it? she wondered desperately. Could she kiss him? Oh, God, how she wanted to! A shiver moved down her spine and she closed her eyes, tipping her face to his, determined to try.

His lips were butterfly-light as they brushed hers the first time. Velvety-smooth as they finally settled over hers. She trembled, bracing herself for the familiar panic, but instead the most glorious sensations spun through her head and swirled to every extremity. He shifted, angling his body, and his knee bumped hers, the pressure only adding to the sensations already churning inside her.

Lips, knees, their fingers still joined. The knuckle beneath her chin. Those were the only parts of their bodies that touched, but every nerve in Sam's body burned as if he'd completely covered her. Slowly he shifted the knuckle from beneath her chin, opening his hand to cup her jaw. His touch was gentle, almost tender and Sam felt tears burn behind her closed lids. Before she could stop them, one slipped onto her cheek, quickly followed by another.

Nash felt the moisture on his hand and pulled back, ending the kiss. He thumbed a tear from her cheek. "I'm sorry. I didn't mean to make you cry."

"No," Sam denied. "It's not your fault. It's—" But how could she explain to him that the tears weren't of regret, but of joy to know that she could kiss him without feeling repulsed, without remembering that awful night.

"Daddy?"

Sam and Nash both turned to find Colby standing in the open door behind them, rubbing sleepily at her eyes. The hem of the T-shirt Sam had given her to sleep in drooped to below her knees and the sleeves hung to her elbows.

Immediately, Nash was on his feet, hauling his daughter up into his arms. "Hey, there, sweetheart. I thought you were asleep."

"I was, but I woke up." She yawned hugely, wrapping

her arms around her daddy's neck and resting her head on his shoulder. "Are we going home now?" she murmured.

"Yes, sweetheart. We're going home." Nash looked at Sam over the top of his daughter's head.

Was that regret in his eyes? Sam wondered. And if it was, was the regret because he had kissed her, or because they had been interrupted? Slowly, unsure of herself, she rose, too, lifting a hand to smooth Colby's tangled hair.

"Do you still want us to come for a lesson on Friday?" he asked uncertainly.

Relief flooded through Sam. "Yes," she replied, then leaned to press a kiss on Colby's cheek. "Sleep tight, cowgirl," she whispered. Another set of lips, male and oh so warm, touched her own cheek. She glanced up to see Nash smiling softly down at her.

"Good night, Sam," he whispered. "And thanks for everything."

Stuffing her hands into her jeans pockets, Sam took a step back and watched as Nash carried Colby to his car.

She lifted a hand in an absent wave while her heart threatened to pound a hole in her chest. "'Night," she called after them. And if her voice was a little breathless, Sam couldn't help it.

She'd finally kissed a man. A handsome man. And she'd survived.

The lesson on Friday was a disappointment to Sam. Not that the lesson itself hadn't gone well. It had. Colby's riding skills were improving daily. But Sam had looked forward to the lesson as a chance to see Nash again.

It had been two days since their kiss and she could still feel the impression of his lips on hers, his taste. She wondered if he'd kiss her again if the opportunity presented itself.

Unfortunately, just before the lesson ended, she'd received a phone call from a neighboring ranch, requesting her veterinary skills in delivering a breech calf.

And so she'd had to cut the lesson short, leaving Nash and Colby behind when duty called.

And now it was Saturday, with three long days stretching ahead of her before she'd see him again. With a sigh, Sam hooked the rope over her saddle horn and swung up into the saddle. But the weekend wouldn't be boring, she reminded herself. They were working calves today on the Double-Cross—castrating bull calves, which promised a calf-fry later that night. And Merideth was due home sometime today for an unexpected, if short, visit. And when Merideth was home, nothing was ever boring.

Sam chuckled, thinking of her sister, then smooched to her horse, guiding him out of the barn and toward the pen where the calves were already churning up dust. Wranglers, mounted and waiting, circled the pen, talking and laughing. Separating the cattle was work, but also a chance for the cowboys to show off their skills both at roping and cutting. Sam felt her own excitement grow.

Mandy had opted to work the chutes and was standing with one hand resting lazily on the release bar, her face tipped up to Jesse's, who was sitting astride Judas, the Double-Cross stallion Mandy had hired him to break when Jesse first returned to Texas. Sam felt the slightest twinge of envy at the sight of them. They were happy. Both of them. And the years that had separated them were all but forgotten.

"Are y'all ready to rodeo?" Sam called out.

Jesse shot her a grin. "Just waiting on you."

"Let's get to work then, before the sun burns a hole in my back."

The cowboys entered the arena in twos, already having drawn straws for partners. Working in teams, they skillfully separated the heifers from the bull calves, sending the heifers down the narrow alley where Mandy caught them in a head chute. Jaime branded them, Gabe gave them their shots, then Mandy set them free into the open pasture.

They worked for hours, the sun rising higher and higher in the sky and turning the arena into an inferno. Dust rose in clouds, collecting in dark lines on facial creases and working its way into the workers' lungs. Sam helped out where she was needed, but hung back, knowing her work would start when the castrations began.

"Hi, Sam!"

Sam glanced over her shoulder to find Colby climbing the fence. Nash stood behind her, peering through the rails. Sam barely recognized him. Gone was the three-piece suit, the starched shirt, the silk tie. Instead, he wore jeans, a T-shirt and boots. Of course the jeans were starched, the boots shined to a mirror finish, and she could swear the T-shirt had been ironed. He even had a gimme hat on his head, advertising John Deere tractors. The overall effect was mouthwatering.

"Well, hi," she said, finally finding her tongue. "What are y'all doing here today?"

"I talked Daddy into bringing me so that I could get in some extra practice," Colby piped up, drawing Sam's attention to her.

"Sorry," Sam said sympathetically. "But I don't have time for a lesson today. We're working cattle."

"We didn't expect you to give her a lesson," Nash hurried to assure her. "She's just wanting to ride."

"Oh. Well, that's fine with me. Did you—"

"Hey, Nash!" Jesse called out as he rode over to the fence to join them. "Are you here to do some roping?"

Nash returned Jesse's smile. "Actually, I just came out to let Colby ride Whiskey for a while."

"Chicken," Jesse teased. "Afraid we'll outrope you?"

Nash chuckled, hitching his boot along the bottom rail. "You wish. Truth is, I've got to keep an eye on Colby."

Jesse craned his head around and let out a shrill whistle.

"Hey, Jaime," he yelled to his son. "You ready for a break?"

Jaime dropped the branding iron and dragged a hand across his forehead, obviously relieved to escape any more work. "You bet!" he called back, loping toward Jesse.

"How about you and Colby ride down to the lake and see if you can scare up some fish to go along with our calf fries tonight?"

Jaime's face spread into a wide grin. Fishing was his favorite pastime. "No problem." He cut a glance at Colby, the look all big-brother bravado. "Can you fish?"

"No," she replied shyly.

"That's all right. I can teach you all you need to know. Come on," he called, gesturing for her to follow. "I'll grab my gear and we'll saddle up."

Jesse grinned down at Nash. "Well, there goes your excuse."

"I don't have a horse."

"There's a couple in the barn you can choose from. In fact, my gelding's probably mad as hell that he's missing out on all the fun. Second stall on the right. There's a saddle there, too, and all the tack you'll need." Grinning, he shot Nash a wink. "Cowboy up!" he shouted in challenge and spun his horse around and rode away.

Nervously, Sam gnawed her lower lip, looking uncertainly at Nash. "You don't have to do this," she murmured.

Nash looked up at her and smiled. "As a matter of fact, it might be kind of fun to be in a saddle again." Touching a finger to the brim of his cap, he turned and headed for the barn.

"Oh, Lord," Sam murmured miserably. "He's going to break his neck for sure."

Sitting astride Jesse's gelding, Nash laid the reins on the horse's neck and picked up the rope, shaking out the loop.

It had been years since he'd roped anything, but he figured it was like riding a bicycle. You never forgot how.

Taking a bead on a hitching post near the barn, he circled the loop over his head and let it fly. It hit the ground about two feet short of his target. Chuckling, he mumbled a warning under his breath. "I wouldn't climb on a bicycle any time soon if I were you, Rivers."

Pulling the rope back in, he wrapped it back into a coil, then shook out the loop. With his eyes fixed on the top of the post, he circled the lasso again and let it fly. It sailed through the air, settling cleanly over the post.

Proud of his accomplishment, he squeezed his thighs against the horse's side, retrieved his rope and headed for the arena. By the time he got there, he could see that they were done with the heifers and had started on the bull calves.

Sam waited for him at the gate, her brown eyes filled with concern. That she was worried about him touched Nash, but he was determined not to embarrass her in front of her family. "Ready," he said, smiling. "Give me the rundown on how y'all are doing this."

"Well," Sam said uncertainly. "We work in twos, with one heading and one heeling. You do know what heading and heeling are, don't you?"

"The header ropes the calf's head, the heeler, its hind legs. Right?" he asked, shooting her a teasing grin.

Sam heaved a relieved sigh. At least he knew the lingo. "Yeah. That's right. Since everyone else already has a partner, I guess you'll be mine. Would you rather head or heel?"

"Head, I guess, since I haven't done this in a while." Seeing her concern, he leaned over and gave her a reassuring pat on the back. "Don't worry. I promise to keep my butt in the saddle and out of the dirt."

Her cheeks burning in embarrassment, Sam gave her head a quick nod. "Okay, then, pick your calf."

Nash plucked his rope from his saddle horn and shook out the loop as he headed his horse into the milling herd of calves. Selecting the one he wanted, he worked him away from the others and lifted his rope. The calf darted, but Nash quickly spurred his horse to follow, circling the rope over his head. Letting it go, he wrapped the end of the rope around the horn and turned his horse just as the noose settled over the calf's head.

With a glance over his shoulder, he saw that Sam was right behind him, her rope already sailing through the air. The loop caught the calf's hind legs and she pulled her horse up short, with Nash doing the same. Dropping his reins, he leaped from the horse's back and ran to catch the calf around the middle and throw him to the ground. Sam was at his side, knife in hand. Kneeling, she pressed a knee into the calf's stomach to hold him in place, while Nash lifted his rear legs. She made the cut, pulled the calf's testicles down, sliced, dropped them into a plastic bag tied at her waist, then sprayed antiseptic on the cut.

They both stood, pulling their ropes from the calf's head and legs. The calf bounded away, bawling. Sam released her pent-up breath, wiping her hands down the sides of her jeans. "We did it," she murmured as if she couldn't quite believe it.

Nash grinned and stuck out his hand. "I'd say we make a pretty good team, wouldn't you?"

Staring at him, she gave her hand another swipe before clasping his in hers. "Yeah," she said, her surprise obvious. "I guess we do."

"Who's the good-looking cowboy with Sam?" Merideth asked, one brow arched in appreciation.

Mandy chuckled. "That's no cowboy. That's Nash Rivers—and hands off! He belongs to Sam."

Merideth whipped her head around to stare, her shock obvious. "Sam?"

Mandy's smile broadened as she slung an arm around her sister's shoulder. "Yep, Sam. Though I'm not sure she realizes it yet."

Merideth turned back to the fence to peer through the slats. "Maybe you better explain. *Reader's Digest* version, please. I'm not in the mood for one of your lengthy explanations."

Mandy bit back a grin. Jetlag had done nothing to improve her sister's disposition. "She's giving riding lessons to his daughter. He's a widower and he invited her out to dinner. Is that brief enough?"

Merideth turned slowly. "And how advanced is this relationship?"

Mandy lifted a shoulder and turned to look at Sam and Nash. "It's hard to tell. You know Sam. Tight-lipped. Keeps everything bottled up inside. Still carrying around a lot of emotional baggage from that incident years ago."

"Is she still in therapy?"

"Yes, for almost a year now."

"Is it helping?"

Mandy nodded toward the arena where Sam and Nash sat on their horses, their knees almost touching. "When was the last time you saw Sam let a man get that close?"

Merideth folded her arms along a rail on the fence, her expression thoughtful as she studied her sister's expression. "Well, I'll be," she murmured. "Who'd have ever thought our little Sam would fall in love?"

Nash swung his leg over the horse's back and slid gingerly to the ground. If his knees wobbled a bit, he tried to hide it. Man, he was going to be sore tomorrow! His thighs already burned and his knees felt like mush. And that was without taking into consideration his rear end, which at this point was still thankfully numb.

Catching up the reins, he waited for Sam to dismount.

"Here," he said, reaching for her reins, "I'll put the horses up."

"No, I can do—"

"Sam!"

Sam whirled at the sound of her little sister's voice. "Merideth!" she cried and dropped the reins, running to throw her arms around her.

"Yuck! Get away from me!" Merideth complained, peeling off Sam's hands. "You smell like you've been rolling in cow manure all day."

Sam laughed, but kept one arm draped around her sister's shoulders. "I have. When did you get here?"

Using two fingers, Merideth plucked Sam's hand from her shoulder and slipped gracefully from beneath her arm. "About ten minutes ago," she muttered in disgust as she brushed from her silk blouse the dust Sam had left there. She shifted her gaze and presented Nash with one of her most dazzling smiles. "Who's your friend?"

Sam looked over her shoulder. "Oh, that's Nash. Come on. I'll introduce you."

"Nash, I'd like you to meet my sister, Merideth Mc-Cloud. Merideth, this is Nash Rivers."

Merideth extended a hand, diamonds winking in the sunlight from a bracelet that swung at her wrist. "Hello, Nash," she said, with a sultry smile.

Nash had to swallow hard in order to work up enough spit to reply. Marty hadn't been wrong when he'd described her, he thought fleetingly. She was a knockout. He wiped a hand on the back of his jeans before taking her hand. "Pleased to meet you," he replied. "I've heard a lot about you."

Merideth batted those baby blues at him and Nash felt his knees weaken. "All good, I hope," she replied coyly.

Sam heaved a sigh. "Give the man a break, Merideth," she muttered under her breath. She snatched the reins from

Nash's hands and led the horses to the barn, leaving Nash with Merideth, his tongue all but hanging out of his mouth.

Sam wanted to be mad at her sister, but she couldn't. Merideth had that effect on men. *All* men, no matter what their age or marital status. She tied her horse to the stall gate, then backtracked to Jesse's gelding's stall. Hooking a stirrup over the saddle horn, she unwound the cinch strap, then let the girt drop to dangle beneath the horse while she fed the strap back through the ring.

"Here. I'll do that." Nash shouldered her aside and reached to drag the saddle from the horse's back. Sam stepped out of the way, surprised by his appearance. She'd figured that by now Merideth would have him following her around like a lovesick puppy, the way she did most men.

She'd seen how Nash had looked at Merideth. She'd even seen her brother-in-law, Jesse, look at Merideth in much the same way, and Jesse was a happily married man who was madly in love with his wife. Merideth just had that effect on men.

"She's beautiful, isn't she?" Sam offered quietly.

Nash cocked his head around to look at her. "Who? Merideth?"

Sam dug a toe into the loose dirt in the alleyway. "Yeah."

"She's that all right, and then some." Seeing the—it wasn't jealousy really, more like wistfulness—in Sam's eyes, Nash took a step toward her and cupped a hand around the back of her neck. Startled, she looked up at him. "But not a bit more beautiful than you," he murmured.

Sam felt heat crawl up her neck to stain her cheeks. Embarrassed, she dropped her chin. "I wasn't fishing for a compliment."

Nash pressed a knuckle to her chin, forcing her head back up. "No, you wouldn't. That's part of your charm."

Then, to Sam's utter amazement, he dipped his face and

pressed his lips to hers. It wasn't a passionate kiss, not by most women's standards, she was sure. But she felt the heat in it burn through every nerve in her body. She closed her eyes, wanting to absorb every sensation, every second of this unexpected pleasure, and when he ended the kiss, she was left breathless and weak. Her eyelashes fluttered up and she found him smiling down at her.

Before she could catch her breath, she heard laughter and the sound of footsteps coming toward the barn. Quickly she shifted away from Nash.

"There y'all are!" Mandy called out. "The kids just returned from the lake and have a nice string of catfish to add to our dinner tonight. We're hoping Nash and Colby will join us."

"We wouldn't want to impose," Nash began.

"Impose my foot!" Mandy cried in dismay. "You both earned your supper."

"Well," Nash said hesitantly. "I'm not sure what Nina has planned."

"I'll call her," Mandy replied, not willing to take no for an answer. "In fact, I think I'll invite her to join us."

Nash and Sam shared a worried look. "All right," he replied slowly. "If you're sure it's not an imposition."

Mandy ended up sending Gabe to fetch Nina, and Sam held her breath waiting for the two to arrive, not at all sure if Nina would be pleased about the invitation.

But no one worried more than Nash. He prayed Nina would be on her best behavior and that she wouldn't create any ugly scenes. When at last he saw Gabe's truck on the long drive leading to the house, he rose from his lawn chair, prepared to greet her.

Colby beat him to the draw.

"Nina!" she screamed, racing for the truck. She had the passenger door open before Gabe came to a full stop. "I'm so glad you're here!'' She caught her grandmother's hand and tugged her from the truck.

Nina adjusted her dress over ample hips. ''Didn't see that I had much choice,'' she muttered, casting Nash a dark look. ''And this man,'' she complained, shooting a glare Gabe's way, ''has a lead foot. I'll be lucky if I didn't suffer a whiplash due to his poor driving.''

Accustomed to her grandmother's complaints, Colby ignored them and grabbed her hand, dragging her to the patio where the others were gathered. ''I went fishing with Jaime and we caught catfish for dinner and I helped clean them and everything!''

Nina looked down at her in a mixture of disgust and dismay, but before she could begin her familiar lecture on girls not being allowed to do such things, Colby stopped, looping her arm through her grandmother's.

''These are my friends,'' she said proudly. ''That's Jesse and Mandy,'' she said, pointing to the couple working at breading the catfish. ''Mandy's Sam's sister and Jesse's Mandy's husband,'' she explained, then turned a bit. ''And that's Merideth. She's Sam's sister, too. And guess what?'' she whispered, tipping her face up to grin at her grandmother. ''She's a movie star!'' She tugged Nina forward. ''And this is Jaime.'' The hero worship in her voice was hard to miss. ''He's Sam's nephew and Mandy and Jesse's son.''

Mandy, always sensitive to others' feelings, must have noticed the overwhelmed look on the woman's face, for she stepped forward, wiping her hands on her apron. ''Hello, Nina, and welcome to the Double-Cross.''

Nina accepted the hand extended to her and managed a nervous smile. ''Thank you. Is there anything I can do to help?''

''Do you know anything about preparing calf fries?''

Nina's brows shot up. ''You mean mountain oysters? Oh, my goodness! I haven't eaten mountain oysters in

years, but I think I remember my mother's recipe. She
added a few extra spices to the breading mixture. A little
garlic, I believe, and a pinch or two of cumin.''

Mandy laughed, catching Nina's hand in hers. ''You've
just been elected head chef.''

Nash watched them walk away and let out a long breath.
Maybe the evening would work out after all.

If Nash hadn't witnessed it with his own eyes, he
wouldn't have believed it. Nina dancing the two-step. And
with Gabe, no less. She'd complain later, he was sure, that
the man had two left feet, but he could see the gleam in
her eye and knew that she was having a good time. Maybe
this is what she needed, he thought on reflection. She rarely
went anywhere except with him and Colby. Perhaps spending time with other people, and people closer to her own
age was what she needed to distract her from her grief.

With a sigh, he stood, looking around for Sam, thinking
to ask for a dance. But he didn't see her anywhere.

''Looking for Sam?''

Nash turned at the sound of the sultry voice, to find Merideth standing behind him. Dressed in ivory silk slacks and
a tunic top of the same color, she stood out from the others
like a pearl in a sea of blue denim. ''Yes, as a matter of
fact, I am. I was going to ask her to dance. Have you seen
her?''

''She slipped off to the barn a few minutes ago. Said
something about checking on one of the horses who suffered a cut on his leg this afternoon.''

Nash smiled. ''That would be Judas. A calf kicked him.''

Merideth eased closer. ''Since Sam isn't here, you could
dance with me.''

Though tempted, Nash realized that it wasn't just any
woman he wanted to hold in his arms. It was Sam.
''Thanks. But I think I'll see if I can help Sam out.''

The offer of a dance had been a test, and Merideth was

relieved that Nash had passed it. She teased him with a smile. "I'm sure she'd appreciate *all* the help you can give her."

The suggestion behind the comment made Nash chuckle. "Can't blame a man for trying."

Turning, he headed for the barn. The lights were off, but that didn't surprise Nash. Sam could doctor a horse blindfolded if necessary. He stepped into the barn, and waited a moment for his eyes to adjust to the darkness. He didn't see Sam, but he heard her soft crooning coming from one of the stalls ahead.

"Sam?" he whispered, in deference to the quietness.

"In here," she whispered back.

A stall door opened and she stepped out, dusting off her hands. "I was just checking on Judas."

"Is he okay?"

"Yeah. It's just a bruise. I put some liniment on it to take care of any soreness."

Nash stepped closer, liking the way the moonlight played on her features. "Dinner was excellent. I really appreciate your family's hospitality."

Sam flapped a hand. "No problem. There's always room for a few more at our table."

"Just the same, I appreciate it." He stepped closer, catching her hand in his. "I was looking for you, hoping to ask you for a dance."

Sam stiffened. Dance? She hadn't danced in years. More than ten, to be exact. "I'm not much of a dancer," she hedged.

"That's okay, I wasn't really wanting to dance." He caught her other hand and pulled her toward him. "I was just looking for an excuse to hold you." He dropped her hands to slip his own around her waist.

"You were?" she asked, her eyes as large as half-dollars as she peered up at him.

"Yeah, I was." He tightened his arms, pulling her closer.

"I like the way you feel," he murmured against her hair. "The way you smell."

Sam snorted, pressing her hands against his chest, sure that he was teasing her. "I'm sure I smell real nice right now. Horse liniment has a real fragrant bouquet."

"You smell wonderful," he insisted, rubbing his cheek against her hair. "Like honeysuckle."

His cheek brushed hers and Sam couldn't help relaxing against him. She rather liked the feel of him, too. Damn, but she could get used to this. There was a comfort in being held so close, and an overall feeling of security that she couldn't remember ever experiencing before.

Gathering her courage, she eased her hands to his shoulders and then over them to rest on his back. Muscles bunched and corded and she couldn't resist smoothing her hands across them, marveling at the strength she sensed there.

"But it's your taste I like best," he murmured, teasing her lips with his. "I could easily become addicted."

His tongue darted out, tracing the shape of her mouth with an infuriating slowness, and electrical shocks ricocheted through Sam. "Yeah, me, too," she muttered, framing his cheeks between her hands, impatient to taste him, as well. She closed her mouth over his, sipping at his lips. "Beer," she whispered. "And maybe a touch of coconut from Mandy's pie." She pressed her mouth more firmly over his and he groaned, pulling her closer.

But close was simply not close enough. Nash nudged her toward the wall, catching her hands in his. Stretching them above her head, he leaned into her, and closed his mouth over hers, drinking deeply.

Sam stiffened, the blood in her veins turning to ice. Images pushed at her from every direction, a nightmare chipping away at reality. She felt the heat of the body pressed against hers, the roughness of the wall against the back of her hands, the mouth that threatened to suffocate her.

Reed Wester. He was going to rape her.

Tears burned behind her closed lids while a scream built in her throat. A hand slipped to her breast, hot fingers burning through the fabric of her blouse. A thumb grazed her nipple and she felt her lungs turn to fire. She had to get away from him! Lifting her boot, she brought it down hard on his instep. With a howl, he dropped her hands, leaping back to hop on one foot, while cradling in his hand the one she'd stomped.

"Jeez, Sam!" he cried. "What did you do that for?"

With her breath coming in ragged gasps, Sam stood staring at him, slowly bringing him into focus as the edges of the nightmare receded...and realized that it was Nash, not Reed who'd held her.

With a strangled sob, she whirled and ran from the barn.

Six

"Sam! Wait!" Nash started after her, but a hand grabbed him from behind, stopping him. He whirled as fingernails dug into his skin.

"What did you do to her?" Merideth demanded angrily.

"Nothing! We were just kissing and she—I don't know," he said helplessly, remembering the fear in her eyes, the wildness. "She just went crazy."

Merideth dug her nails a little deeper. "Did you force yourself on her?"

Nash's mouth sagged open. "Of course not! I only kissed her."

"Have you kissed her before?"

"Yes," he replied, beginning to resent the inquisition. "A couple of times."

"So what was different about this time?"

Nash frowned, trying to think over the events. "She seemed more aggressive. It was when I backed her up against the barn wall that she went a little crazy."

Merideth groaned, dropping his arm. "I was afraid of this."

"Afraid of *what?*" Nash asked in growing frustration.

Merideth turned her gaze toward the far end of the barn where Sam had disappeared. "This is where it all happened."

Nash dug his fingers through his hair, knowing somebody was crazy and fearing it was him. "I wish to hell you'd tell me what you're talking about. I haven't a clue."

Merideth lifted a brow and looked at him. "She hasn't told you?"

"Told me *what*, for God's sake?"

Heaving a sigh, Merideth took his arm and led him to a line of hay stacked against the wall. Pressing a hand to his chest, she forced him to sit, then sat on the bale next to him. "Sam was nearly raped."

Dumbfounded, Nash stared at her then dropped his face to his hands. "Oh, my God, no," he moaned.

"When she was eighteen," Merideth continued. "One of the ranch hands attacked her late one night when she was coming in from a rodeo. He knocked her up against the wall there, pinned her hands above her head and tried to rip off her clothes. When she screamed, he dragged her into a stall, and would have raped her, if Gabe hadn't heard her and come running."

The scene she described was so damn close to the one he'd just made Sam suffer through, Nash could understand why she'd panicked, why she'd run. "Oh, my God," he mumbled.

"That's not all."

He cocked his head to look at Merideth, wondering what more could possibly have happened to Sam.

Merideth sighed and plucked a piece of straw from the bale to twist between her fingers. "Daddy died that same night. He came to the barn to see what all the commotion was about and when he discovered that Gabe had fired the ranch hand, he was furious. To make a long story short, he suffered a massive heart attack and died. Even though we all knew that he had high blood pressure, Sam blamed herself. Somehow all of this—the near rape and daddy's death—twisted itself around in Sam's head and she's never recovered from it."

Nash had heard enough. He bolted to his feet. "I've got to find her. Talk to her."

"She may not want to see you. She'll be embarrassed."

"She may not want to see me, but I *have* to see her. Oh, God, Merideth, do you realize what I've done to her?"

"No, I can't imagine," she replied slowly, watching him closely. "But you may be the only one who can help her right now." She stood, brushing straw from her slacks, hoping her instincts to trust him were correct. "Try the old smokehouse down at the foot of the hill. She used to hide out there when we were kids and she was upset."

Nash cursed himself with every step he took. He should have known something was wrong. He should have been more sensitive to Sam's behavior. Now that he knew what had happened to her, the signs were all there, warning lights that he should have picked up on from the very first. The swagger and bluff she used to hide her femininity. Her reluctance to let him get near her, to touch her. Her nervousness the night he took her to dinner. The fact that at her age she didn't seem to have ever dated. Her innocence the times he had kissed her.

He worried if he'd be able to find her, if she'd even talk to him if he did. And what would he say to her? "I'm sorry that I treated you so roughly? That I reminded you of a night you'd rather forget?"

He dragged off his cap and slapped it against his leg. Sorry? Sorry didn't come close to expressing how low he felt.

Before he reached the smokehouse, he heard her. A high,

keening sound, followed by a gut-wrenching sob that froze him in midstride. He was tempted to turn right around, head back to the house and send one of her sisters to see to her, but he knew he couldn't. He was the one who'd brought back the memories. He was the one who'd made her cry.

Slapping the cap back on his head, he strode for the smokehouse's low door. He pushed it open and stuck his head inside. "Sam?" he called softly. When she didn't answer, he stepped inside, closing the door behind him. Though the building hadn't been used in years, the scent of smoked meat still hung in the air. A portion of the roof was missing and moonlight poured through the gap.

He saw her huddled in a corner, the moonlight ending at the toes of her boots. Her knees were pulled to her chest, her face pressed against her folded arms. He crossed to her, dropping to a knee in front of her, and stretched out a hand. She shrank away and he caught himself just shy of touching her.

"Sam, I'm sorry," he murmured.

She drew herself into a tighter ball of misery. "Go away," she sobbed.

"No." He sat down on the ground, clasping his hands around his own raised knees to keep from reaching out for her again. God, how he wanted to touch her, to pull her onto his lap and just hold her, to soothe away her tears, her fears. But he knew that having him touch her was the last thing she would want right now.

"I didn't know," he said helplessly.

She stiffened, but kept her face pressed against her arms. "Who told you?"

"Merideth."

She groaned, burying her forehead deeper into her arms.

Again he reached for her, but caught himself, slowly curling his hand into a tight fist of frustration. "I'm not like him, Sam," he whispered, wanting, needing to reassure her. "I would never hurt you." He sensed more than saw the shudder that racked her shoulders. "Oh, Sam," he murmured, and this time he couldn't stop the hand that reached to cup the back of her neck. "Please, Sam, don't cry anymore."

"I—I can't help it," she sobbed brokenly. "I'm so ashamed."

"Ashamed?" Stunned, he dipped his head, trying to see her face. She wasn't angry with him? He shifted his hand from her neck to her chin, gently forcing her tearstained face up to his. "Why? You have nothing to be ashamed of."

She shoved at his hand and scrambled to her feet, away from him. "Oh, don't I?" Her eyes gleamed with fury as she glared down at him. "How many women do you know who can't have sex, who can't even get near a man without feeling as if they are suffocating?"

"But not all women have suffered through what you have," he reminded her gently.

"And how does that change anything?" she demanded angrily. "I'm still half a woman. I can't even kiss a man without going ballistic on him."

Nash rose slowly. "You've kissed me, Sam."

"Yeah," she muttered dryly, raking her fingers through her hair and turning away. "And look how that ended."

"Not every time," he reminded her. "Tonight in the barn was my fault. I pushed when I should've gone slower. Had I known—"

"And how would knowing have changed anything?" she cried, wheeling to glare at him. "*I'm* the problem here, not you."

"I would have been more gentle, more understanding. Sam," he added softly, taking a cautious step toward her, "I wasn't trying to force myself on you. You've got to believe me. I just wanted to get closer. Do you have any idea what you do to me? How you make me feel? You're a beautiful woman, filled with a sensuality that I don't think you even realize you possess. When you wrapped your arms around me and kissed me, I wanted to crawl inside you. I wanted to feel every lush curve of your body against mine. You make me ache, Sam. You make me burn. *You,* Sam," he added with emphasis. "I've never wanted a woman more."

His words shocked Sam, the sensual pull of them moving through her, making her blood warm, her knees weak. He wanted her? Even after what had just happened in the barn? No, she told herself, stiffening her spine. She couldn't allow herself to believe him. She'd learned the hard way not to trust men.

He took a step nearer, daring to take her hand in his. When she didn't pull away, he pressed it against his chest. "Feel that, Sam? That's my heart. Can you feel it beating?"

"Yes," she whispered weakly, feeling the impression of each of his fingers against her hand, the swell of his chest beneath her palm. She stood spellbound, mesmerized by powerful gray eyes and the throbbing of a heart that matched her own.

"That's what you do to me. I want you. And I think you want me, too," he added, his voice dropping to a husky whisper in the dark smokehouse.

She swallowed hard, wanting to deny the claim. But she couldn't. She did want him. In spite of what had happened in the barn earlier. She'd lain awake at night for weeks, dreaming of lying in his arms, naked and writhing beneath him, touching him, kissing him, feeling the strength, the hardness of him inside her.

But those were only dreams. The reality was different. Thanks to Reed Wester, she'd never know a man in that way.

Her shoulders drooped and her hand slipped from beneath his on his chest. "It's no use," she murmured in defeat. "I can't."

"You can," he insisted, stepping closer, determined to prove to her that she was wrong. "Touch me, Sam. Anywhere you want. I know you want to. And I swear I won't touch you back unless you ask."

The challenge was there in his voice, the sincerity of his promise obvious in the depths of his gray eyes. Sam believed him. But could she do what he asked of her? Oh, God, how she wanted to!

Tentatively, her fingers trembling, she raised a hand and placed it on his heart. Its pounding reverberated through her palm while the heat from his body melded with her own. She stared at the back of her hand, waiting for the fear to come, the panic. But nothing happened. Slowly, she lifted her gaze to his. Heat shimmered in the moonlight between them.

She lifted her other hand, splaying it across his chest and feeling his muscles tighten in reaction, seeing the heat build in his eyes. "I want to feel you," she whispered, "your bare skin."

His gaze never moved from hers. "It's your call. Do what you want."

Sam swallowed hard, her eyes shifting to his T-shirt. He really was leaving all this up to her. Slowly she moved her hands to his waist and tugged the hem free from his jeans. Hauling in a deep breath, she pulled the fabric upwards. He raised his arms and bent at the waist, allowing her to pull the shirt over his head. Then he straightened and braced his hands at his hips, waiting, unmoving.

Moonlight danced and shadows played across the swells and valleys created by muscles on his upper body. A mat of soft, dark hair swirled across his chest. A neat six-pack, barely visible in the dim light, gleamed with a fine sheen of perspiration. The dark hair appeared again at his navel, just visible above the waist of his jeans, and then disappeared beneath starched denim. She'd dreamed of him naked like this. But her dreams hadn't come close to the reality. She lifted her hands to his chest.

Nash felt as if his skin was on fire. It took every shred of willpower he possessed to remain still, to refrain from dragging Sam into his arms and taking her right there, right then on the smokehouse floor. But he knew how important this was. For Sam, as well as himself. He'd promised, and he'd damned well make good on that pledge. In spite of his determination to remain rigid, unmoving, a slight shiver shook his body when her fingers inadvertently grazed his nipples.

She jumped back, clasping her hands behind her back, her eyes wide with alarm as she lifted them to his.

"It's okay," he reassured her gently. "Just a reflex."

At the sincerity she saw in his eyes, she stepped closer again, reaching up to frame his face with her hands. His mouth stretched into a smile beneath her trembling palms, a day's growth of beard scraping against her hand. "You can kiss me, if you like," he murmured, hoping to tease some of the fear from her. "I won't bite."

And kissing was exactly what was on Sam's mind. Unable to resist, she rose to her tiptoes and lifted her face to his. The taste was there—beer and coconuts—just like in the barn. Sighing, she eased closer and her breasts nudged his chest.

He groaned, but didn't move. "I sure would like to put my arms around you right now," he murmured against her lips.

Sam stiffened, then forced herself to relax. This was Nash. He'd promised. And so far, he'd honored that pledge. "Okay."

His arms closed around her, gently drawing her nearer. She was aware of each finger that touched her waist, caressed her spine, and the strength in the forearms that brushed the sides of her breasts. But his touch remained light, gentle.

"Is it okay if I kiss you back?"

His request blew warm and moist against her mouth, teasing her lips open. "Yeah," she murmured and lifted her arms to circle his neck.

His tongue traced her lips from corner to corner, then he settled his mouth over hers on a sigh. The absolute tenderness beneath the kiss drew tears to her eyes.

Nash felt the moisture against his cheek. "Oh, Sam, don't cry," he murmured, forgetting his promise and drawing her closer.

"I'm not," she lied.

He drew back to eye her suspiciously.

"Well, at least not for the reason you think," she murmured in embarrassment.

His eyes softened in understanding. "Then how about kissing me again?"

In answer, she lifted her face and their lips touched briefly, then again, and again until their mouths molded together.

Passion. It had a flavor, Sam realized dreamily. She'd never known. And a texture. Silky satin and coarse velvet. Color, too. Vibrant reds, soothing blues. Anxious to discover more, she deepened the kiss and Nash responded, slipping his tongue between her parted lips. His gentle probing stroked a fire to life low in her abdomen, a fire that quickly rose to burn in her chest. Every nerve in her body seemed to burst into flame. Never had she felt more aroused, more like a woman.

She pressed herself more firmly against him, hungry for the feel of his body against hers. He shifted, slipping a thigh between her legs. Startled, she tensed, then relaxed when he did nothing more. Then slowly, he began to sway, rubbing against her femininity, denim chafing against denim, and pleasure shot through her in glorious waves. The pressure of his thigh increased, the heat inside her building and building until she thought she'd surely explode. His hands moved at her back, kneading, spreading to encompass her waist, then sliding upwards to press against the sides of her breast. She needed something…what, she wasn't sure, but surely relief of some sort before she died.

"Nash?"

"What?" he murmured, dragging his mouth from her lips to nibble at the smooth column of her neck.

"I need…"

"What?" he asked again, his voice husky. "Tell me what you want."

"Touch me," she all but begged.

"Where?"

She took his hand and pressed it to her breast. "Here."

His hand closed over her breast, his fingers gently kneading. "Like this?" he murmured against her fevered skin.

"Yes!" she gasped, arching.

Nearly blind with his own needs, Nash slipped his hand inside her blouse and she arched even more, straining for his touch. He caught her turgid nipple between his fingers and rolled it between them. He felt the tension building in her body and knew she was near flash point. He could give her this, he told himself, and take nothing for himself, to prove to her that she could trust him, to prove that she was capable of being with a man and not knowing fear.

Tearing his hand away, he lowered his face over her breast, warmed it with his breath, then closed his mouth over it, drawing it deeply into his mouth. He felt the tension move through her, heard her sharp intake of breath. Her fingers dug into his shoulders and her legs squeezed like a vise around his thigh. She dropped her head back with a low guttural moan…and came apart in his arms.

Nash sank to the hard floor, drawing her with him, cradling her on his lap while shudders racked her slim body. Finding her lips, he pressed fervent kisses against them, her face, murmuring soft, soothing words to her.

Her eyes fluttered opened, her gaze meeting his in the

moonlight. "I never knew," she whispered. "I never knew it would be like this."

Nash smiled down at her, catching a tendril of hair from her face and tucking it behind her ear. "Trust me. It gets even better."

Her cheeks reddened, and he felt himself lose a little bit more of his heart to her. "I'm sorry," she murmured. "You didn't—"

Nash pressed a finger to her lips, then replaced it with his own. "Sshh. Let's just take this one step at a time."

Mandy and Merideth stood on the edge of the patio, staring off into the darkness. Mandy's foot tapped a staccato beat on the bricked patio, while Merideth remained still, the picture of calm. Inside, she was wound tighter than a spring.

"I can't stand this not knowing," Mandy said in frustration. "I'm going after them."

Merideth caught her arm, jerking her back. "You are not," she said firmly. "Nash can handle Sam."

Mandy turned her head to scowl at her sister. "And what do you know about Nash Rivers? You met him for the first time today."

Merideth folded her arms beneath her breasts, her expression smug as she turned her gaze again to the darkness. "Yes, but I know men, and I can assure you, Nash can handle anything Sam throws his way."

"He better handle this well, or, by God, he'll have to answer to me," Mandy replied grimly.

"Answer to *us*," Merideth corrected. She draped her arm around her older, but shorter sister. "The Three Musketeers, remember? All for one and one for all."

Mandy bit back a smile. "Yeah. I remember." Then the smile disappeared as her mouth sagged open. "Look!" she whispered, pointing. "Is that them?"

Merideth squinted her eyes, watching as Nash and Sam

stepped from the shadows near the barn. They were holding hands. Smiling, Merideth tucked her arm through Mandy's and hustled her toward the house before Sam could see them. "I told you Nash could handle her."

Mandy craned her head back over her shoulder as Merideth dragged her away, trying to get a glimpse of Sam's face to make certain that her sister was all right. Was that a flush of pleasure on Sam's face? she wondered in surprise. And didn't her blouse look a little rumpled?

Smiling a secret smile, she turned her head and allowed Merideth to drag her the rest of the way to the house. "Maybe," she said, not wanting to concede a win to Merideth just yet. Her sister's ego was already way too big.

Sam leaned to pull a jug of milk from the refrigerator and felt two pairs of eyes boring into her back. She turned to find Merideth and Mandy standing in the kitchen doorway.

Mandy pasted on an overly bright smile. "Good morning, Sam. How did you sleep last night?"

Eyeing her sister warily, Sam scuffed to the table and plopped down in a chair. "I slept okay." She dumped cereal into a bowl, then added milk. When her sisters continued to stare at her, she set the jug of milk on the table. "What is it with you two?" she asked suspiciously.

Merideth breezed across the room, a cloud of silk billowing around her shapely legs. She leaned to pat Sam's cheek as she might have patted a child's. "Nothing, darling," she said airily, and slipped onto the chair next to Sam. "We were just concerned."

Narrowing an eye, Sam scooped up cereal. "About what?"

Before Merideth could answer, Mandy dropped down in the chair across from them and resumed her inquisition. "Did you have fun last night?"

Sam shifted her gaze to Mandy's, her frown deepening. "Yeah. I guess so. Why?"

"Oh, I was just curious. Nash seemed extremely attentive. In fact, I noticed that y'all disappeared for a while."

Sam felt heat crawl up her neck. Surely they didn't know. How could they? Did she have a sign on her forehead that read, "I just experienced my first climax, and, boy, was it a doozy!"

"He's nice to everybody," she replied vaguely. "He's that kind of guy."

"Yes," Merideth agreed on a dreamy sigh, "and sexy as hell. That body!" She fanned her face with her hand. "I'll bet he's one heck of a lover."

Sam decided to leave that one alone.

Mandy leaned across the table, peering at Sam intently. "Don't you think he'd be a good lover, Sam?" she prodded.

Sam dropped her spoon in disgust. "Would you two just cut it out? Jeez, is nothing sacred around here?"

A smile bloomed on Mandy's face. "You did, didn't you?" She clapped her hands with glee. "I knew it! I just knew it!"

"You don't know anything," Sam grumped. When they both continued to peer at her knowingly, she shoved back her bowl. "Okay, so we played around a little, but my virginity's still intact. Are you satisfied now?"

"Details," Merideth pressed, leaning closer. "We want details."

Sam shoved back her chair and rose. "If you want details, read a romance. I've got to go." She turned, grabbing her hat from the counter and ramming it on her head.

Mandy looked at her, her face slack with disappointment. "Go where?"

"To Austin. Colby's running in her first competition today. I'm hauling Whiskey and meeting her there."

"Will Nash be with her?" Mandy asked hopefully.

"Yeah," she muttered, fishing her keys from the pocket of her jeans. "So what?"

"So-o-o-o," Merideth repeated dramatically, "maybe you'll have a chance to play around some more."

"It's a horse show, Merideth," Sam grumbled, "not an orgy."

Sisters. Who needs 'em? Sam thought with disgust as she brushed Whiskey's coat. Nosy little busybodies, always trying to mind her business for her. And she could have done without their little interrogation this morning. Her nerves were already pretty much shot. She'd stayed awake most of the night thinking about what had happened with Nash, thrilling at it, then worrying about having to face him again today. What was a woman supposed to say to a man after sharing something so intimate with him? How was she supposed to act?

With a groan, she tossed the brush into the tack box. It clattered against the metal side, and Whiskey jumped sideways at the unexpected noise, rolling his eyes. "Sorry," she muttered, giving him an absent pat. "Didn't mean to scare you."

"Do you think he understands you?"

The voice was so close to her ear, Sam felt the moist warmth of it against her neck. And it was familiar, too, the huskiness of it sending a shiver chasing down her spine. Nash. Turning her head slightly, she found him standing behind her, smiling, that dimple teasing her, and she wondered how she could have ever dreaded this moment. Slowly, her nerves unwound and she smiled back at him. "It's the tone that soothes him more than the words." She glanced over his shoulder. "Where's Colby?"

"She stopped at the rest room. I think she's a little nervous."

"That's normal."

"For fathers, too?"

Laughing, Sam couldn't resist giving his cheek a reassuring pat. "Yeah, fathers, too."

Before she could remove her hand, Nash caught it in his and drew it around his neck, pulling Sam close. "I couldn't sleep last night," he murmured, hooking his arms around her waist.

"Me neither," Sam whispered, transfixed by the warmth in his gaze.

"I was thinking that maybe later, we could—"

"Sam and Nash, sitting in a tree, k-i-s-s-i-n-g. First comes love, then comes marriage. Here comes Nash pushing a baby carriage."

Not having heard Colby come up behind her, Sam widened her eyes in alarm. But the fact that his daughter had caught them in such an intimate embrace didn't seem to concern Nash—or at least not in the way it did Sam.

He merely groaned, dropping his forehead to rest against hers. "She's a cute kid," he murmured woefully, "but she's got lousy timing."

The *later* Nash had mentioned never came. The day was spent either preparing Colby for a run, caring for Whiskey, or watching the other riders compete. The only time they had been alone was when Colby herself was in the arena competing, but then their attention had been focused on her and not on each other.

Sam sighed as she climbed into bed, exhausted after the long day, but a little frustrated, too. She'd really been curious about that *later.* She leaned to switch off the light, then tucked her hands behind her head and stared at the ceiling, sleep the last thing on her mind. Now that she'd had a taste of what sex was like, she was ready to experiment a little more.

She choked back a laugh. For a woman who'd avoided intimacy for more than ten years, she sure was getting bold. She wondered what Camille would have to say about that.

She closed her eyes, envisioning Nash, remembering the night before. The gentle way he had talked to her and soothed her, the tenderness in his touch, the understanding with which he had listened to her and dealt with her fears. She loved him.

Her eyes flipped open wide. Loved him? She brought a hand to her heart, trying to still its rapid beating. Slowly the words sank in. It's true, she thought in awe. She did love him.

The phone rang, and Sam leaned over to grab it. "McCloud Veterinary Service," she said, wondering what emergency awaited her at this late hour.

"Sam?"

She sank back against her pillows, a smile building as she recognized the husky voice. "Nash?"

"None other. Did I wake you?"

"No. I'd just climbed into bed."

"What are you wearing?"

Her smile deepened as a warm flush washed over her body. "Why do you want to know?"

"Just curious."

She glanced down at the faded T-shirt and wished she could lie and say a skimpy silk teddy. "Nothing sexy, if that's what you're wondering."

"Let me be the judge of that."

"A T-shirt," she mumbled, more than a little embarrassed.

"How long is it?"

Frowning, Sam kicked off the covers and stared down at her legs. "It hits me about mid-thigh."

"Are you wearing anything under it?"

Because she wasn't, Sam's eyes widened and her mouth dropped open. "Nash!"

He groaned. "No, don't tell me," he said miserably. "It'll only make things worse."

"Make what worse?" she asked hesitantly, her nerves dancing to life beneath her skin.

"I can't get you off my mind. I can't sleep for thinking about you."

Sam pulled the covers back over her legs and hugged them to her chin as she snuggled deeper into the pillows. "Me neither," she admitted shyly.

"Want to meet me?"

Sam's fingers tightened on the receiver. "When?"

"Now."

"Now?" she repeated, her heart almost thudding to a stop.

"Yes. Now. Look out your window, Sam."

Frantically, Sam kicked back the covers and scrambled from the bed. Holding the phone tight against her ear, she whisked back the drapes and pressed her nose to the window. Sure enough, Nash's Mercedes was parked on the drive out front. The tinted window on the driver's side glided down and his face appeared. He smiled, his cellular phone pressed against his ear.

"Hi, Sam," he murmured, his voice husky.

Sam had to swallow before she could find her tongue. "H-hi," she stammered in return.

"I like your T-shirt."

She dipped her head, staring down at her shirt as if seeing it for the first time. Self-consciously, she tugged at the hem.

"What does it say?"

Sam immediately straightened and slapped a hand across her breasts, gathering the words into a fist, her cheeks flaming. "Nothing."

The car door opened and he swung out a leg, then stood, still holding the phone at his ear. While Sam watched, staring at him in horror, he crossed to her window. Only a thin pane of glass separated them. "Move your hand, Sam," he said into the receiver. "Let me see what it says."

"No," she said, trying her best to cover the words printed on the shirt and hang onto the phone at the same time. "It's just something silly."

"Then come outside."

She stared at him through the window, her heart skipping a beat. "Now?" she whispered into the receiver.

"Yes, now. Hang up the phone, Sam, and unlock the window."

Her movements almost robotic, Sam placed the receiver on its base and raised her hands to unlatch the window. Nash stuffed his own phone into his back pocket, then lifted the sash. He leaned inside, holding out his hand.

Hesitating only slightly, Sam placed her hand in his, then sat on the windowsill and swung her legs over. With a tug, Nash had her standing in front of him. He held her at arm's length and lowered his gaze to her shirt. "Cowgirls need loving, too," he read. He lifted his gaze to hers, a brow arching into his handsome forehead. "Is that a fact?"

Mortified, Sam dropped her gaze. "It's just a silly shirt. Merideth gave it to me as a joke."

"I'm not laughing."

Sam slowly lifted her head, her gaze meeting his. Heat turned his gray eyes to smoke.

"Everybody needs love, Sam." He pulled her closer, wrapping his arms around her. "I've wanted to do this all day," he murmured, hugging her tight against him. "And this," he added, finding her lips with his.

There was no slow buildup of passion, the heat was there waiting for them, the by-product of a long day of suppressed need. Sam melted against him. "Oh, Nash," she murmured, lifting her arms to curl her hands around his neck. Her movements added a new angle, a new depth for him to explore. He took what she offered, careful to keep his actions slow, nonthreatening.

But Sam didn't want slow. She'd waited all day for this. Heck, she'd waited her whole life! There was no fear—

well, maybe a little—but mostly just a yearning, an anxiousness to know what she'd been missing. She dug her fingers into his hair, drawing his face closer. With a groan, Nash slipped his tongue between her parted lips and dropped his hands to her buttocks, arching her against him, pressing his hardness against her pelvis.

"Where can we go?" he whispered urgently.

Sam tried to clear the webs of passion from her mind so that she could think clearly. Certainly not her bedroom. Merideth was right next door and would surely hear them. Nash's car? No, way too confining. "My trailer," she whispered. "There's a changing room up front that has a bed."

Seven

Catching her hand, Nash tugged her along behind him, toward the barn where the trailer was parked.

A rock on the drive dug into Sam's bare heel as she jogged to keep up. "Ouch!" she cried, hopping on one foot. Nash paused only long enough to swing her up into his arms, then strode on. At the trailer, he shifted her weight to a lifted knee and opened the side door, stepping quickly into the dark interior and closing the door behind them. He stopped, unable to see so much as his hand in front of his face.

"Is there a light?" he whispered.

"To the left of the door."

Nash hit the switch with his elbow and a small light flickered on. It didn't offer much more illumination than a night-light, but in its soft glow, Nash saw the raised platform and the bare mattress on top of it. He crossed to it and gently sat Sam on its edge. She immediately grabbed the hem of her T-shirt and stretched it over her knees.

The action served to remind Nash of her inexperience, her innocence, the need for caution. He rested his hands on her thighs and stepped closer, gently wedging his hips between her knees until he stood in the gap between her dangling legs. He felt the tremble of her flesh, saw the glimmer of nerves in her wide brown eyes. "We don't have to do anything you don't want to do," he assured her.

Sam hauled in a deep breath. "No. I want this...y-you," she clarified, and silently cursed the quiver in her voice.

His eyes remained on hers while he slid his hands down, catching the hem of her T-shirt and easing it up over her knees, her thighs. "I want to see you," he whispered, his voice husky. "All of you."

At her hips, he paused, allowing Sam to make the decision. She hesitated only a moment before she shifted, allowing him to ease the T-shirt from beneath her, then lifted her arms so that he could slip it over her head. Though the temptation was strong to cover herself, Sam forced her arms to her sides.

"Beautiful," he whispered reverently, lifting a hand to cup a small breast. "Absolutely beautiful." He let his hand drift down, smoothing it across the flat plane of her abdomen until the heel of his hand bumped her feminine mound.

Sam wasn't sure if it was his words or his touch that stroked the fire to life low in her abdomen. But it didn't matter. She didn't want to think, to analyze...she just wanted to feel. Closing her eyes, she let her head drift back with a shuddery sigh.

His hands, clever, but gentle, roamed her stomach, shaped her hips, then slithered down to mold her thighs. The very tips of his fingers traced their length, drifted over her knees...then disappeared.

"Open your eyes, Sam," he ordered gently.

Heavy-lidded, she complied, her gaze meeting his in the soft light.

"I'm going to undress, but I don't want to frighten you. I thought it might help if you watched."

Before she could respond, he toed off his boots, his hands moving to unbuckle his belt, unzip his jeans. Her mouth suddenly dry, Sam wet her lips, but her eyes remained fixed on his hands and the bulge just visible behind them. Catching the hem of his shirt, he tugged it free of his jeans, then slowly, starting at the bottom, began to release each button. A triangle of bare flesh appeared. A swirl of dark hair. Then dark blue silk. Sam swallowed hard, as her gaze settled on the swell of manhood jutting beneath the silk fabric. Slowly, she lifted her gaze to his.

He saw the desire in the depths of her brown eyes, but he saw the fear, too, and it was the fear he responded to. "Any time you want me to stop," he told her, "just say the word and I will."

Watching her carefully, monitoring her reaction, he shucked the shirt from his shoulders, let it hang there a moment, giving Sam time to adjust to the sight of his bare chest, then dropped the shirt to the floor. Keeping his movements slow, he hooked his thumbs in the waist of his jeans and pushed them down, slowly stripping the fabric down his legs. Once free of them, he kicked them aside. He stood, his hands braced at his hips, wearing nothing but a pair of blue silk boxers and a smile.

Sam stared openly. "Wo-o-o-w-w," she murmured.

The word was out of her mouth before she realized she'd voiced it aloud. *Wow?* She gave herself a swift mental kick. How juvenile! How utterly stupid! Surely she could come up with a better word than "wow" to describe such a perfect male specimen! At the sound of Nash's chuckle, she felt her cheeks warm, but couldn't for the life of her find the courage to look him in the eye.

Sensing her embarrassment, Nash moved to stand between her legs again. He framed her face with his hands and tipped it up to his. "My sentiments exactly," he whispered, dropping his hands to her shoulders and holding her in place while he took his gaze on a slow journey down her body. "Wow," he said, giving a lusty sigh.

He couldn't have done, said, anything that would have put Sam more at ease. Laughing, she caught his face between her hands and drew his mouth to hers.

Edging her back, Nash sank a knee into the mattress between her legs, levered himself up and followed her down, bracing himself above her. Slowly, carefully, he lowered himself over her, letting her take more and more of his weight, letting her feel the heat, the friction of flesh rubbing against flesh. All that separated them was blue silk and Nash was beginning to resent even that small barrier.

Tearing his mouth from hers, he raised his head to peer down at her. "I want to make love to you, Sam. Will you let me?"

Her eyes never once wavered from his. "Yes," she whispered. "I want that, too."

Angling himself, he leaned over the side of the bed, nabbed his jeans and fished in his pocket, removing a gold packet. He rolled away from Sam and to his back, breaking open the seal.

She closed her hand over his and sat up. Nash felt the tremble in her fingers and lifted his gaze to hers, sure that she'd changed her mind, that she couldn't go through with this.

"Let me," she said softly, taking the packet from him. Surprised by her sudden boldness, Nash watched as she shifted to her knees to catch the waist of his silk boxers in her hands. She pulled them down his legs, inch by slow aching inch, and dropped them over the side of the bed. He felt the tremble of her fingers as she placed the condom over his manhood and had to grit his teeth at the featherlike touch of her fingers brushing against his hardness as she smoothed it into place.

His breaths came shorter and shorter, his lungs burning, his loins crying for relief.

"Sam," he gasped, catching her waist in his hands and pulling her over him. "You're killing me."

"Good," she murmured, smiling seductively. "That makes us even."

On a groan, Nash pulled her face to his, taking her mouth in a plundering kiss that stole her breath. He rolled, pinning her beneath him. With his knees, he spread her thighs, creating a nest for himself. "I don't want to hurt you, but I might." He warned her. "But it'll only hurt for a minute."

"I know," she said, "it's okay."

His fingers found her petaled opening and slowly spread the velvet folds while his lips found hers again. Teasing her with his tongue, he stroked her, preparing her. He felt the heat build in her, the impatience, until finally she arched, rising to meet him.

With a moan, he sank down, pressing his arousal against her honeyed opening, gently seeking entry. She bit back a cry at the first slow thrust, pleasure and pain warring for dominance...but then it was only pleasure...and an urgency that grew inside her until she was sure she would explode.

He began to move, and she caught the rhythm of his movements, felt his passion and answered it with her own. Perspiration beaded his back beneath her hands while she urged him on. Faster and faster, racing through the night. "Nash," she gasped, digging her fingers into his back. "I—"

He rose, bracing his hands on either side of her, his gaze focused on her, and thrust one last time, burying himself deeply inside her. She sucked in a sharp breath, arching hard against him. He felt her stiffen beneath him, watched the passion wash over her face, glaze her eyes...then she shattered, her hot, velvety flesh pulsing around him. Then, and only then, did he allow himself his own release.

"Sam," he murmured, gathering her in his arms. "Oh,

Sam,'' he whispered and rolled, bringing her with him and cradling her to his chest.

He lay there, weak and trembling, while her heart threatened to jackhammer a hole in his chest. A shudder racked her slim body. Concerned, he scraped her hair back so that he could see her face. "Are you okay?"

"Yes," she murmured, cuddling close. "More than okay." She lifted her head, a smile spreading on her flushed face. "Can we do it again?"

Dawn pinkened the sky through the narrow window above the bed, but Nash only had eyes for Sam. Curled against his side, she slept, her fingers laced between pillow and cheek. Her hair draped over a shoulder and partially concealed a breast. An angel. She looked like an angel.

He shook his head, remembering his first impressions of her. A woman who dressed like a down-on-his-luck cowboy, one who could be as prickly as a porcupine when cornered, a woman who could ride and throw a rope better than most men...well, she wasn't quite the woman he'd first thought her to be.

As he looked at her now, he saw an angel. Innocent. Delicately boned. Utterly feminine. Slowly, he shook his head again. No, she was no angel. Not when it came to loving. She was a seductress, passionate and demanding, while at the same time generous and giving. And she was a hell of a fast learner.

Keeping his touch light, he caught the hair that shadowed her face and tucked it behind her ear. She sighed and shifted closer. Nash felt his groin tighten in response.

How had this happened? he asked himself. Why had he come to her last night? Was it to seek closure for that first night in the smokehouse? Then his thoughts hadn't been on his pleasure, his own needs. His actions had been purely unselfish, his thoughts focused on Sam and her needs, her pleasure. He'd desperately wanted to help her, to make her realize that not all men were the same. He'd wanted to prove to her that she wasn't half a woman, that she was filled with passion just waiting to be released. He'd wanted in some way to make up to her for the hell he had put her through by his callous actions.

But last night was different. He hadn't come to her out of any sense of guilt. And his actions had been anything but unselfish. He'd needed her, wanted her more than he'd wanted any woman in his life.

As he stared down at her, remembering the pleasure, the passion they'd shared, he felt his heart soften and grow warm. Could he be falling in love?

His breath came out on a shuddery breath. Love. He hadn't thought himself capable of experiencing that emotion again. Not after what Stacy had put him through. But he couldn't deny the feelings that were pressing against his chest. The man who shared nothing of his personal life with anyone suddenly had an overwhelming urge to share it with Sam.

"Sam?" he whispered.

Her eyelashes fluttered and she slowly opened her eyes. A dreamy smile played at her lips. "Ummm." She snuggled closer, but closed her eyes again.

"Come on, Sam," he urged, "wake up. I want to take you somewhere."

"What's the rush?" she murmured sleepily, blinking open her eyes to peer at him.

"I've got something really big that I want to show you."

Sam slipped her hand between their bodies and took him into her hand. "I hate to disappoint you, Nash," she said, a slow smile tugging at her lips as she stroked him. "But I've already seen it."

Her playful teasing caught him by surprise, but it was the clever movements of her fingers on him that tripped a wire, making his need to hurry seem less urgent. He rolled, bringing Sam across his chest. Just one more taste, he promised himself, then he'd take her and show her his dreams.

Her smile spread, lighting her eyes with mischief as she braced her hands against his chest and gazed down at him. "I thought you said we needed to hurry?"

"Forget what I said," he growled, catching her lower lip between his teeth. He clasped his hands at her hips to guide her to him. "We've got all the time in the world."

Sighing her pleasure, Sam closed her mouth over his as he entered her. The heat was instantaneous, spreading through her womb, burning away whatever inhibitions remained and leaving her with a confidence she'd never thought she'd possess. She was a woman now in every sense of the word and she had a woman's needs, a woman's desire. Lacing her fingers with his, she drew his arms above his head and held him there, then lifted her head to meet his gaze. Heat danced between them. "I want you," she whispered and began to move, her eyes locked on his. "All of you."

And all of him was what Nash was prepared to give her. "Then take me," he replied, his voice rough with his own need as he arched his hips high to meet her. He thrust deep inside her, filling her with his hardness, and nearly lost his fingerhold on control when she sank down, taking him even deeper. Passion glazed her eyes, slackened her grip on his hands...and then she began to ride him. Faster and faster until perspiration glistened on her skin and her face was flushed with the effort. When he was sure he couldn't hold back any longer, she arched, crying out, and curled her fingers into fists around his hands. With one last thrust he sent them both tumbling over the edge.

"So when are you going to tell me where you're taking me?"

Keeping his gaze on the road, Nash reached across the

console and grabbed Sam's hand, dragging it to his thigh. "I'm not. It's a surprise."

"Meanie," she muttered halfheartedly.

Chuckling, he slung an arm along the back of her seat and drew her as close as the bucket seats would allow. "So Colby tells me."

Biting back a smile, Sam gave his thigh a squeeze and settled back for the ride. She couldn't remember the last time she'd ridden in a car with a man. Other than Gabe and Jesse, of course. More often than not when out on the ranch, she found herself squeezed between the two of them in the cab of the truck.

But it had never felt like this. This was special. Intimate. She could feel the swell of muscle on Nash's thigh, the heat that burned through his jeans and into her hand. The weight of his arm on her neck wasn't a burden, but a comfort, one she hadn't dared to believe she'd ever experience.

"We're here."

His announcement drew her from her thoughts and she sat up just as they passed under the faded and rusted sign that proclaimed Rivers Ranch.

"Oh, Nash! We can't go to your house! It's barely morning! What will Nina and Colby think?"

"Don't worry. We aren't stopping at the house. I just want to show you my plans for the property."

Sam sank back with relief as Nash swung the car onto a dirt path barely visible through the tall grass and weeds.

"Along the highway frontage will be a strip shopping center," he explained. "Fast food, convenience store, dry cleaners, that type of thing. Here," he said pointing, "is where the residential lots begin. Most are five acres, but we do have a few that are closer to ten."

They bounced along with Nash pointing out different features of each of the lots, sharing his dreams. Sam could hear the pride in his voice, the excitement, but as she looked around her all she felt was an overwhelming sadness.

"And this will be the golf course," he finished, waving a hand at the acreage in front of them. "Arnold Palmer is designing it for me."

"What did you raise here?" Sam asked, trying her best to envision a golf course where cattle or horses should be grazing.

"Herefords. Dad was real proud of his herd."

"What happened to them?"

Sam felt his shoulder rub against hers as he shrugged. "I sold them." Swinging the car around, Nash headed back to the entrance. "Now I have another surprise for you."

As they drove, Sam looked around her, imagining the land being used as it was meant to be. Cattle grazing on thick green grass. Horses running across the wide meadows, their manes and tails flying in the wind. Birds singing in the trees. Ducks swimming in the ponds.

They bumped their way onto the main highway and Nash turned right, headed toward Austin. But Sam's mind was still focused on Rivers Ranch. She could understand why Colby was fighting so hard to stay there. It was a beautiful place, peaceful and full of promise. How could Nash *not* want to live there? She could understand his feelings about his career, but just because he lived on the ranch didn't mean he had to be a rancher. Lots of people owned farms and ranches but worked in Austin, hiring a manager to take care of their livestock and the daily chores. Why couldn't Nash? This was his heritage, for heaven's sake! His family had worked there and died there. Surely that must mean something to him!

"Well, what do you think?"

His question pulled Sam from her dismal thoughts. "About what?"

He pulled his car to the curb and parked, leaning around Sam to point. She turned to follow the line of his finger.

They were parked in the middle of a cul-de-sac, and a two-story stucco condo with a postage-stamp-sized lawn stood on the other side of the curb.

"This is my house," he explained proudly. "The one we're going to move into as soon as Rivers Ranch subdivision is underway."

Sam stared at the narrow building, at the less than twenty feet that separated it from the units on either side and felt a shiver chase down her spine. She couldn't imagine living in such cramped quarters, not after spending her whole life on the Double-Cross, where she had hundreds and hundreds of acres to roam. Not that the condo wasn't nice. It was obviously expensive, and probably very roomy inside.

"I'd show it to you, but I don't have the key with me," Nash said with regret.

Sam let out a slow breath. "That's okay. Maybe another time."

Nash dropped a quick kiss on her cheek. "Yeah. Another time."

As they drove back to the Double-Cross, Sam's mood sank lower and lower. She loved Nash and she suspected that his feelings for her were the same. Why else would he want to share his plans with her, his dreams? The problem was, Sam didn't share those same dreams. How did two people go about blending their dreams, their lives, when they were so different?

"Sam, look," Nash said, giving her shoulder a nudge with his. "Is that smoke?"

Sam pushed her worrisome thoughts aside and peered through the windshield ahead. Her eyes widened. "Oh, my God! Something's burning."

"At the Double-Cross?"

"No! It's too far away for that. It has to be the Circle Bar. We've got to tell Jesse."

Nash raced to the Double-Cross but when they reached the house, Sam pressed a hand against his arm. "His truck's gone," she moaned, her worried gaze scanning the drive. "He must already know."

Nash whipped the car around and headed back down the drive.

Sam sat on the edge of the seat, her gaze focused on the wall of black smoke billowing against the morning sky. "Oh, God, please don't it let be the barns," she murmured, her thoughts centered on the defenseless livestock she knew were penned there.

Hearing the fear in her voice, Nash stretched out a hand, lacing his fingers with hers. "It's probably nothing more than a load of hay that's caught fire," he offered, trying to reassure her. "You know how much those suckers smoke."

But when they topped the hill that looked down on the valley where the Barrister home lay, they both sucked in a shocked breath. Flames leapt from the roof of the Georgian-style home and curled from the shattered windows, licking upwards. "Oh, my God, no!" Sam cried.

Nash pressed the accelerator to the floor, racing toward the burning house. Trucks were parked helter-skelter across the lawn in front, while men ran, dragging hoses from the volunteer fire truck and adding them to those already aimed on the house.

Before the car came to a complete stop, Sam was leaping out and racing toward the crowd who watched helplessly from a safe distance. Spotting Mandy, Sam grabbed her sister's arm. "Where's Jesse?" she gasped.

Her face creased with worry, Mandy nodded toward the barns. "He and Pete are moving all the horses out into the pasture, just in case it spreads."

"Margo?" Nash asked, joining them. "Did she get out?"

Before Mandy could answer, Nash heard the high-pitched wail. He craned his neck to see above the crowd and saw Margo, still dressed in her nightclothes, racing toward the house. A fireman grabbed her, pulling her back.

"My house!" she screamed, fighting to break loose. "I've got to save my house!"

Though the faces of those who looked on were sympathetic, no one made a move to console her. Nash remembered Sam telling him that Margo had few friends. None among the wranglers who worked the Circle Bar, none among the neighbors who had gathered to offer their help in putting out the fire.

Feeling duty-bound by their business relationship to offer what comfort he could, Nash started pushing his way through the crowd. "Here, I'll take her," he told the fireman and took a firm hold on Margo, turning her away from the destruction. "Margo," he soothed. "There's nothing you can do now."

She collapsed into his arms. "Oh, Nash!" she sobbed, clinging to him. "My house. My beautiful house. It's ruined!"

"I know, Margo, I know," he murmured, trying to calm her. "But you can build another one, even finer than this one."

She pushed from his arms, her eyes wild. "No!" she screamed. "I can't! It was all in Wade's will. If the house was ever destroyed, the land it stands on reverts back to the estate. It's Jesse's now! Jesse's!"

The venom behind the name wasn't lost on Nash. Nor was the attention her screams were drawing from the crowd. Out of the corner of his eye, he saw Sam pushing her way toward him and was grateful for her support when she joined him.

"Why don't you let us take you somewhere?" Sam offered gently, laying a hand on Margo's arm. "Someplace where you can rest."

"You sumuvabitches," a male voice yelled drunkenly. "Git yore hands off'n me."

The crowd parted, revealing Jesse and Pete striding forward, dragging a man between them. Soot camouflaged the parts of the man's face his hat didn't shadow.

Sam felt tension shoot through Margo's arm just before the woman jerked free of her.

"You!" Margo screeched, turning on the man. "You did this to me!" She flew at him, her nails scraping against his face, her fists battering his chest.

He lifted his arms to ward off her blows and inadvertently knocked off his hat. Sam's eyes widened in shock as his face came into full view. Though his eyebrows were gone and his hair was singed to a frayed mass of black, she recognized him. "Rube," she whispered in disbelief.

Nash turned to her, frowning. "Who?"

"Rube. He used to work on the Double-Cross. Mandy fired him when he threatened to whip Jaime." She gasped, grabbing for Nash's arm as Margo succeeded in landing a blow on the man's chin. Rube staggered back, cradling his chin in his hand while a snarl curled his lips.

"You bitch," he spat out. "I didn't do nothin' to you that you didn't deserve. You were supposed to pay me, remember? A sweet little deal. All's I had to do was provide you information on the goings on over at the Double-Cross between him," he said, jerking his head toward Jesse, "and that whore of a woman he now calls his wife."

At the word "whore", Jesse grabbed Rube by his collar and jerked him upright, thrusting his face up close to his. "Don't you ever let me hear you refer to my wife in that way again." He gave the man a rough shake. "You hear me?"

Rube's adam's apple bobbed convulsively, his eyes wide with fear. "Y-yeah, I—I hear you."

Jesse angled his head, turning his dark gaze on Margo. "Is what he said true? Were you paying him to spy on us?"

Margo took a step back, her eyes wide. "N-no! He's lying."

"I ain't lyin'," Rube yelled. "She paid me twice. Over six months ago. It was the last time she wouldn't pay up on. I was to call her and let her know when you and the kid and—" he swallowed nervously, obviously concerned about Jesse's threat "—and yore wife got back from that camp-out y'all went on jist 'fore you got hitched. I told her I was gonna make her pay one way or t'other."

"So you set her house on fire," Jesse finished for him.

"No! No! I swear! I was jist gonna scare her a bit. You know, put the fear of God in her. But I tripped and dropped the can of gasoline and it went sliding across the porch. When I went to grab for it, my cigarette fell outa my mouth and—"

Jesse tightened his hand on Rube's collar. "You fool. You're lucky you didn't blow yourself to kingdom come. I ought to kill you myself."

Another man pushed through the crowd, this one dressed in a uniform. "I'll take it from here," the sheriff offered, slapping cuffs around Rube's wrist.

Nash had to hold Margo back as the sheriff dragged Rube away. She finally sagged, weak and defeated, in his arms. "He's ruined me," she moaned. "He's ruined me."

Jesse turned to glare at her. "That's what you get when you play with fire, Margo. You get burned." With one last scathing look, he turned and headed back to the barn, Pete trailing him.

"It's all the McClouds' fault," Margo wailed, needing to put the blame somewhere, anywhere but where it belonged...with herself. "They are the ones responsible for all this trouble."

At the insult, Sam's spine stiffened. "The McClouds had nothing to do with this."

Margo whirled on her. "Oh, yes, they certainly did. If your sister had left Jesse alone, he would have sold me the Circle Bar and gone back to Oklahoma where he belongs. But, no!" she said bitterly. "She had to woo him, just like she did years ago when she got pregnant with that bastard son of hers.''

Sam thinned her lips, her anger building. She wouldn't listen to Margo demean her family in such a vile way. She grabbed the woman's arm. ''This time you've gone too far, Margo.''

Margo jerked free of her. ''What are *you* doing here, anyway? Did you come here to gloat? To laugh while my home, my life went up in flames?''

Nash stepped between them. ''No, she came out of concern. I brought her.''

''You?'' Margo fell back a step, stunned. Then her eyes narrowed as she took in his rumpled clothing, the shadow of a day's growth of beard. ''You're sleeping with her, aren't you?'' Before he could either deny or acknowledge the accusation, Margo lifted her chin imperiously, chilling him with a freezing glare. ''I refuse to do business with anyone who associates with the McClouds. You'll end it now, or I'll remove every cent I have invested in the Rivers Ranch project. And I'll take the other investors with me. You'll be ruined. And it'll be all *her* fault,'' she accused, stabbing a finger Sam's way.

The threat was a blow that slammed into Sam's heart. She staggered back a step, then spun around and pushed her way through the crowd.

Nash felt the rage swell. ''To hell I will,'' he said in an angry whisper. ''Sam means more to me than your precious money.'' He whirled to follow Sam, but Margo grabbed his arm, her fingernails biting deep into his arm.

''I want my money now!'' she raged.

He spun, glaring at her, and jerked free. ''You'll get your money when I'm damned good and ready to give it to you.''

He turned and pushed his way through the crowd, searching for Sam. As he broke through the other side, he saw the truck from the Double-Cross driving away.

Sam was behind the wheel.

"I don't want to talk about it."

Merideth and Mandy shared a concerned look over the top of their sister's head. "But, Sam—" Mandy began.

Sam lifted her head from the drawer she was digging through. "I said, I don't want to talk about it," she repeated firmly. "End of story." She snatched a T-shirt from the depths of the drawer and jerked it over her head. "I've got to go," she muttered, and pushed past them, slapping a cap on her head.

"Where?" Mandy cried.

"The Cowans. I've got to test their cattle for Bangs."

She strode from her bedroom, leaving her sisters behind.

Mandy turned to Merideth. "What are we going to do?" she cried.

Her arms folded beneath her breasts, Merideth tapped a polished nail against the satin sleeve of her robe. Though she'd missed all the action, Mandy had filled her in on the details, scant as they were, while Sam showered. "Nothing," she finally said, and returned to her room to resume her packing.

Mandy trailed her. "But we have to do something. Sam loves him. I know she does."

"If she does, then she'll talk to him, not us. You can't push Sam into doing anything. You know that as well as I do."

The doorbell chimed and Merideth called out, "I'll get it." She set her suitcase in the entry and opened the door, expecting to find the driver for the limousine she'd ordered.

But it was Nash who stood on the opposite side of the door, his hands braced against its frame.

"I need to talk to Sam."

The smell of smoke still clung to his clothes, his hair.

The fact that he looked like he'd been to hell and back tugged at Merideth's heart. "She's not here."

"Where is she?"

"I don't know," Merideth lied, though she knew very well that Sam was at the Cowans' testing their cattle.

"I need to talk to her."

"I don't think she wants to talk to you right now. Give her some time, Nash. She'll come to you when she's ready."

Nash buried his face in his hands. Two weeks. Two weeks of calling and leaving messages on Sam's machine. Two weeks without a reply. He'd gone to her house three times, trying to see her. But her family had formed a formidable wall of protection around her, refusing to let him inside.

She'd even had Gabe haul Whiskey back to the Rivers Ranch, removing even that small thread that still connected them. Gabe hadn't said two words to him when he'd delivered the horse, though he had stayed on at Nina's invitation to share a glass of lemonade with her on the front porch.

Nash groaned, pressing his face harder against his hands. If only he'd followed her home, he told himself, maybe things would have turned out differently. But he'd been so furious with Margo, so ready to be rid of her, that he'd driven straight to his office, written her a check for her investment and delivered it to her personally, all but shoving it down her throat.

He didn't need Margo Barrister or her damned money. There were plenty of investors who'd love the opportunity to invest in his project.

But there was only one Sam.

He had seen the stricken look on her face when she'd turned away. And he knew he had to talk to her, to soothe away the ugliness Margo had painted on their relationship. Desperate to do just that, he'd raced to the Double-

Cross, but by the time he'd made it, Sam had gone and Merideth refused to tell him where.

She missed him. And Colby. So much that her heart ached like a strained muscle that no amount of massaging would help. She loved Nash. But how could she do anything that would harm him or make him unhappy? She knew how much the River Ranch project meant to him. She'd heard the excitement and pride in his voice when he'd driven her through the property, sharing his plans with her. Though she didn't agree with what he was doing with his inheritance, his heritage, she wouldn't let her presence in his life take his dreams away from him.

But oh, God, how she missed him.

Swallowing back tears, she dumped onto the counter the box of vials she'd prepared for her next call and reached for her bag.

The phone rang and Sam snagged the extension in the barn. She tucked the receiver between shoulder and ear and began to stuff the medication into her bag. "McCloud Veterinary Service."

"Oh, Sam, thank goodness I caught you!"

Sam tensed at the urgency in the woman's voice. "Nina? What's wrong?"

"It's Colby," Nina sobbed hysterically.

Sam tossed aside the vials she was holding and closed her fingers around the counter, fear gripping her heart. "What's happened? Is she hurt?"

"No, at least I don't think so. She's in the loft in the barn and she refuses to come down. She swears she'll jump if I come near her. I've called and called, trying to find Nash, but I can't locate him. Oh, please, Sam," she begged. "You've got to help me."

"I'm on my way."

Eight

Sam parked by the barn doors and leapt down from her truck, looking around for a sign of Nina or Colby, but not finding a trace of either.

"Hi, Sam."

Sam raised her head, shading her eyes with a hand at her brow. Colby sat in the opened doorway to the loft above her, her feet dangling over the side. Sam swallowed back the fear that lodged in her throat. "Hey, Colby," she said, trying to hide the panic in her voice. "What're you doing up there?"

"I'm on strike."

"Really? Can I strike, too?"

Colby lifted a shoulder. "Sure. Why not?"

Sam ducked inside the barn and made a beeline for the stairs that led to the loft. When she stuck her head through the opening and saw Colby leaning out the window looking down, she had to squeeze her hands into fists around the ladder's side rails to keep from tumbling right back down.

"Colby?"

The child twisted her head around, peering at Sam over her shoulder. "Yeah?"

"Honey, could you move away from the edge a little bit?"

Colby glanced down, then looked back at Sam again, frowning. "Why?"

Sam forced herself to climb the rest of the way into the loft. She pressed a hand to her middle as her stomach threatened to revolt. "I'm afraid you might fall."

Colby grinned. "Did Nina tell you I was going to jump?"

"Well," Sam replied vaguely, "she might have mentioned that."

Colby twisted back around, swinging her legs, her heels thumping against the side of the barn. "I just told her that so she'd leave me alone."

Though that should have comforted Sam, it didn't. Her stomach continued to swirl as she looked beyond Colby and saw nothing but blue sky.

Darn it! Why couldn't Colby have locked herself in her room or something? Why did she have to choose the loft? Sam had this thing about heights. She couldn't help it. Ever since she was a kid, she'd suffered the malady, and no amount of teasing or cajoling would make her climb anything higher than her head. Swallowing hard, she tried again. "How about if you scoot back just a little?"

Colby turned to look at her again, her brow furrowed. "You're scared aren't you?"

"No—well, maybe a little."

"There's nothing to be scared of. You aren't going to fall." She waved Sam on. "Come over here. The view is great."

Though it took every bit of willpower she possessed to do so, Sam took that first step. Then another, and another, until she was standing just behind Colby. She sank to the floor, closing her eyes against the dizzying sensation. "Why are we striking?" she asked weakly.

"They delivered all the equipment today to start cutting the roads." Colby leaned again, pointing. "See? It's over there by the road."

Sam grabbed for the tail of the child's T-shirt and hung on for dear life, but turned her head away, unable to look. "Yeah, I saw it all when I drove in. So what does that have to do with our strike?"

"I don't want them cutting the roads. If they do, then it won't be long before we have to move."

So that was it. Sam heaved a sigh of relief. At least the kid wasn't suicidal.

"Prisoners strike all the time," Colby explained. "They refuse to eat until the warden meets their demands."

"And you're demanding that your dad put a stop to the development of Rivers Ranch?"

"Yep. And I'm not coming down until he promises. Daddy never breaks a promise."

No, he doesn't, Sam thought, feeling a stab in her heart.

Touch me, Sam. Anywhere you want. And I swear I won't touch you back unless you ask.

And he hadn't touched her, even though she knew now how difficult that must have been for him.

"No, he doesn't break promises," she admitted slowly, her heart breaking all over again. "He's a good man."

Colby turned to her then, looking at her quizzically. "Why are you mad at my daddy?"

Stunned, Sam could only stare. "I'm not mad at him."

"He said you were and that was why you weren't going to give me any more lessons. He said you won't even return his phone calls. He said—"

A horn blasted and Colby whirled again to the open window. "Uh-oh," she murmured. "Daddy's home."

Sam felt her own stomach plummet at the news. She didn't want to see Nash. She didn't think she could bear the pain.

"And, boy, does he look mad."

"Colby Renée Rivers, you get yourself down here right this minute!"

Sam found the courage to peek out the window. Nash stood below, his hands fisted at his hips, his mouth set in a dark frown.

"No! And you can't make me," Colby yelled back. "Sam and me are on strike!"

Nash's face went slack. "Sam? She's up there with you?"

Sam inched closer, raising her head above Colby's so that he could see her. "Yeah, I'm here. Nina called me."

His gaze met hers for an instant, a split second in which Sam thought she saw pain and regret. Then he shifted his gaze to Colby, his frown returning. "Well, both of you climb down or I'm coming up!"

"Quick, Sam!" Colby whispered. "Get the ladder!"

Sam scrambled across the floor to the loft and heaved the ladder up, straining under its weight…then cursed herself for letting Colby sucker her into this. "Colby, this is ridiculous," she muttered as she crawled back to her. "If he wants up here, he can get up, with or without the ladder."

Colby narrowed an eye, peering down at her father. "Yeah, but it'll slow him down while we come up with a plan."

"What plan?" Sam asked in frustration.

"I'm not sure yet. I'm still thinking."

"Colby," Sam began, striving for reason. "Do you really think that your dad is going to knuckle under to your demands? This is his business, for heaven's sake. He can't just quit!"

Tears brimmed in Colby's eyes and her lower lip quivered. "But I thought you were on my side, Sam. I thought you'd understand."

Her heart breaking, Sam gathered the girl close. "I am, sweetheart. And I do understand." She eased Colby to arm's length, cupping her hands at the child's shoulders. "But we can't always have what we want, no matter how badly we want it."

Sam knew, because she wanted Nash. So badly that she could hardly stand it. But she also knew she couldn't have him.

Tears slipped from Colby's eyes and slid miserably down her cheeks. "I don't want to move, Sam. I like it here."

"I know you do, sweetheart." Afraid that she'd cry herself, Sam drew in a long, shuddery breath. "Let me talk to him," she suggested softly. "I'm not promising anything, you understand. But I'll see what I can do."

Colby threw her arms around Sam's neck. "Oh, Sam! Thank you! He'll listen to you, I just know he will."

Slowly removing herself from Colby's embrace, Sam leaned to peer out the window. "We're coming down," she called out to Nash. "You can call off the National Guard."

It angered Nash that Sam could crack jokes when his heart was threatening to split wide open. Steeling himself for the confrontation, he paced to the door of the barn and waited.

First Colby, then Sam appeared in the doorway. Unable to look at Sam, Nash focused his anger on his daughter. "Colby Renée Rivers, I ought to turn you over my knee right now and blister you good. Do you have any idea the trouble you've caused? Nina is about to have a stroke, and you've made Sam drive all the way out here when I'm sure she's got better things to do with her time."

Sam stepped forward, placing a hand on Colby's slim shoulder. "I came because I wanted to," she told him firmly. "But I'd like to talk to you, if that's all right."

Startled by the request, Nash looked at her a moment before asking suspiciously, "What about?"

Ignoring his question, Sam gave Colby a light shove. "Go on to the house and check on your grandmother. This shouldn't take long." Colby obeyed, but turned when she'd passed her daddy's line of vision and shot Sam a thumbs-up sign.

In spite of her nervousness, Sam had to bite back a smile at the child's impudence.

"I've missed you, Sam."

The unexpectedness of the admission grabbed at Sam's heart. "I've missed you, too, Nash." The words were out before she could stop them. "And Colby," she added hastily.

"Then why haven't you returned any of my calls?"

Sam felt the tears coming, and turned away. She didn't want to relive this. The first time had been painful enough. "It's not important."

Nash grabbed her elbow, whirling her back around and forcing her to look at him. "It *is* important. Or at least it is to me. Damn it! I love you, Sam."

Sam dropped her chin to her chest, unable to meet his gaze. If she did, she was afraid she'd tumble into his arms. "Listen, Nash. I really appreciate what you did for me. You—" Embarrassed, she heaved a deep breath. "Well, you took away my fear of intimacy, and for that I'm eternally grateful."

Frightened by her refusal to look at him, Nash tightened his hold on her. "Sam, what are you saying?"

"I'm saying that there's no future for us."

At one time, Nash hadn't thought so either, but he suspected Sam's reasons might be a whole lot different from his. "Why?"

"Look at you, Nash," she said, pulling free to gesture at him. "Three-piece suits, Italian loafers. And look at me," she continued, throwing her arms out from her sides. "I'm a country girl, a veterinarian who slogs through cow manure all day. We're like oil and water. We just don't mix."

His face reddened, a muscle tensing on his jaw. "I think we mix just fine."

"Physically, yes. It's our lifestyles that don't mesh."

Because there was truth in what she said, Nash pressed his lips together, unable to form a comeback.

"I've known it from the first, but I ignored it. But when Margo said what she did—"

"Is that what this is all about? Margo?" He grabbed her arms, forcing her to face him. "Don't you realize that you mean more to me than some crazy old lady's money?"

Sam stared, unable to believe she'd heard him correctly, then she gave herself a hard shake. It didn't matter what he said. She'd made her decision. She wouldn't stand in the way of his success. She couldn't. The guilt would eat her alive.

Besides, she was here to fight Colby's battles, not her own.

"Does Colby mean that much to you, as well?" she asked.

He dropped his hands from her arms. "I can't believe you'd ask me that. You know I love Colby."

"Colby doesn't want to move."

"So what else is new?" Nash tossed up his hands in frustration. "What am I supposed to do? Just shut everything down, give all the investors their money back? Damn it, this is my job, how I make my living. She's just going to have to adjust."

"She's had to do a lot of adjusting in her life. Couldn't you cut her a little slack?"

Nash pressed his fingers at his temples. "Please. No more guilt. I live with enough as it is."

Though she wanted to reach out and comfort him, Sam kept her arms pressed at her sides. She had to do this for Colby. She was the child's only chance. "I'm not trying to burden you with guilt. I'm just trying to make you see Colby's side of this. She lost her mother and she's been uprooted three times already. She's made friends, then lost them with each of the moves. She needs some stability in her life. Roots. Whether you realize it or not, Colby's roots are here, where yours are."

He shook his head, denying her claim. "My roots are where I plant them. So are Colby's."

"Her roots are here," she argued, pointing to the ground beneath her feet. "Haven't you heard anything she's said to you? She's begged you not to divide up the ranch. She pulled up the surveyor's stakes to slow things down, to buy herself a little more time here. This afternoon she even went on strike, threatening not to eat or come down from the loft until you promised to put a halt to your plans. She was ready to battle you for what she wanted, what she needs. Isn't that enough to prove to you how strongly she feels about this place? Her roots are here!"

"Why here?" he cried in frustration. "Why can't she set down roots somewhere else?"

"In the condo you're planning to move to?"

At his defensive look, Sam pressed on. "Colby doesn't want to live in a condo, Nash. She wants to live here, where she can have her horse and ride whenever she wants. Where she can sleep in her daddy's old bedroom. Where memories of her grandparents are easily drawn. Don't take that away from her, Nash. Please, I beg you."

His jaw tensed, a muscle jumping to life there. "You're asking too much."

"Am I?" Sam stuck her hands in her pocket and took a step back. "Maybe you're asking too much of your daughter." Fearing that her heart would break if she stayed a moment longer, she turned and headed for her truck.

"Where's Sam?"

"She went home."

Nina tossed down her dishcloth and set her dripping hands at her hips as she whirled to face Nash. "And you let her?"

"W-well, yeah," he stammered, surprised by her anger. "But I didn't *send* her home, if that's what you're thinking. She said what she wanted to say and then she left."

Nina rolled her eyes. "You've been mooning over the

woman for weeks and when you finally get a chance to talk to her, you let her leave! What you should've done was propose to her.''

Propose to her? This coming from Nina? Stunned, Nash could only stare.

Nina humphed and went back to scrubbing dishes. "Colby needs a mother. I won't be around forever, you know." She cocked her head over her shoulder to look at him. "And you need a wife. It's time you got on with your life. Stacy would want that for you."

Still reeling from his conversation with Nina, Nash knocked on Colby's door, then stuck his head inside her room. She sat on her bed, a large book spread across her knees. Tears dripped from her chin and splatted against the pages.

"Oh, Colby, baby, please don't cry," he said, crossing to sit down on the bed beside her. "Daddy's not mad at you."

"I'm not crying for me," she said, sniffling. "I'm crying for them." She pointed to the page in the book.

Nash looked over her shoulder and saw that it was the Rivers Family Bible spread open across her legs. The page she pointed to was the family tree. Each generation listed was penned by a different hand, births, marriages and deaths all neatly entered. Nash found his own name there, as well as Stacy's and Colby's. Stacy's entry was the most complete of the three—birth, marriage, death all recorded in his mother's handwriting.

Nash wrapped an arm around his daughter, hugging her to his side. "Why, sweetheart? Why are you crying for them?"

"'Cause I know they'd be sad, just like me, if they knew Rivers Ranch was going to get all cut up, and their house torn down."

Nash closed his eyes, and heaved a long breath. "Colby,

we've talked about this a thousand times. I'm not a rancher, I'm a developer.''

"I know that, Daddy. But don't you think it's sad? I mean, look at Sam and her family. They've lived on the Double-Cross their whole lives. They've got pictures and stories and everything, about all the McClouds who lived there before them."

"We have that, too," Nash reminded her. "We have this old Bible, plus we've got all Grandma and Grandpa's photo albums to look at."

"Yeah, but it's not going to be the same once everything changes. This old house won't be here. Whiskey's barn will be gone. There'll be nothing left to remind us of all our relatives who lived here before us. Nothing but pictures, that is." She shook her head sadly. "We won't have a place to come home to anymore. It'll all be gone."

Nash sat in the rocker on the front porch, gently rocking back and forth, Colby cradled in his lap. Fireflies blinked on and off in the distance, while the fragrant blooms of the wisteria teased at his nose. The movement of the rocker was soothing, a comfort after the miserable day he'd had. First the confrontation with Sam, then the conversation with Nina, and finally the tearful session with Colby.

He smoothed a hand along the arm of the chair, finding comfort in the worn wood. His father had made the chairs, years ago, as a gift to his mother. She'd loved sitting out on the porch at night, shelling peas or just dreaming. His father would sit with her, talking, planning out the next day's work. Always work, Nash thought with a sigh. That's what was always paramount in his daddy's mind.

He pushed a foot against the porch floor and set the rocker in motion again, his thoughts drifting lazily as he studied the porch posts and the trailing wisteria that climbed it. How long had that plant been growing there? he wondered. Had his mother planted it, or his grandmother? He wasn't sure, but as far back as his memory

could carry him, the wisteria had been there. He could remember summers when they'd suffered droughts and the
fields would be drying up and turning brown. His mother
would fill a five-pound coffee can with precious water and
carry it out to pour on the plant's roots.

She'd loved the wisteria; the smell of it, the soothing
shade it provided for the porch on a hot afternoon. And
she'd shared that love with Nash. What would she think if
she knew her wisteria was soon to be plowed under, along
with the house she had scrubbed and cleaned and taken
such pride in?

Frowning at his thoughts, Nash took a slow look around.
The porch his grandfather had crafted with his own hands.
The pastures in the distance where Nash had worked along-
side both his grandfather and his father, raking and baling
hay. He could almost see the cattle grazing. The herd of
prized Herefords that they'd bred and nurtured over the
years. He'd sold off the herd when his daddy had died and
thought nothing of it. He wondered now what his daddy
would have thought of his decision.

Nash swallowed back the lump of emotion that rose in
his throat. He supposed it was his conversation with Colby
earlier that had spawned these thoughts.

He shook off the guilt before it could settle for good on
his shoulders. I'm not a rancher, he reminded himself. I'm
a developer. The only use I have for land is to subdivide
it and build on it.

Colby snuffled in her sleep, burrowing closer to his chest,
as if to remind him of her presence and her opinion on the
matter. He looked down at her, his heart twisting in his
chest when his gaze came to rest on the tearstained cheeks,
the puffy eyes.

She was young, resilient. She would adjust, he told himself. She always had before, with each of their moves.

But then she'd always had Rivers Ranch to come home
to.

I'm just trying to make you see Colby's side of this. She

lost her mother and she's been uprooted three times already. She's made friends, then lost them with each of the moves. She needs some stability in her life. Roots. Surely you can understand that?

Sam's words came back to haunt him. A base. Roots. A stable place in an unstable world. Isn't that what he'd always tried to provide for Colby? She was his all, his reason for living. Why would he want anything but the best he could give her?

Colby needs a mother. I won't be around forever, you know. Nina added her own chant to the voices echoing in his mind. *It's time you got on with your life. You need a wife. Stacy would want that for you.*

Stacy. The familiar anger squeezed at his chest. If she had lived, he wouldn't be suffering through all this right now...at least not alone. But she hadn't given a thought to his needs, his desires. She'd wanted a baby and had gambled her life on the chance of having one. He dipped his head, his gaze going to his daughter.

She looked like Stacy. She had her mother's eyes, her stubborn chin, the same color of hair. She had her heart, too. Warm and giving. He'd almost forgotten that trait in Stacy. As he stared at his daughter, she shifted in her sleep, throwing an arm around his neck...and Nash's heart did a slow flip in his chest as realization slowly dawned.

How could he be angry with Stacy? he asked himself. She had given him a gift, the most precious one she could give. She had given him a daughter, Colby, a part of herself that would be with him always. Stacy had known she wouldn't live out a full life, just as Nash had known it when he'd married her. But she'd snipped her life a little shorter in order to leave Nash with this precious gift. Why hadn't he realized this before now?

Tears burned his eyes and he turned his gaze up at the heavens. A star, brighter than the rest, stood out against the black-velvet sky. "Thank you, Stacy," he murmured, his voice thick with emotion. The star seemed to wink at Nash, acknowledging his thanks. Through blurry eyes, he watched it streak across the sky in a blaze of light, then disappear.

Nash awakened, groaning. He sat up straighter in the rocker, shifting Colby to a more comfortable position, trying to stretch out the kinks that sleeping in the stiff chair had placed there. He hadn't meant to spend the night out on the porch, but at some point he must have fallen asleep.

In the distance he heard the sound of a truck and glanced in that direction. Men were already climbing down and striding toward the earth-moving equipment parked near the entrance.

He tightened his arms around Colby. This is it, he told himself. There's no turning back now.

He watched the first bulldozer begin to move, the driver dropping the massive bucket into position for the first cut. He could hear the scrape of metal against the hard-packed earth, the grinding of rock...and felt it as if it was scraping against his skin, grinding at his heart.

He couldn't do this! He couldn't sacrifice the land his father and his grandfather had worked so hard for, the land that they had sacrificed for and bled for. Sam was right. He had roots here, tenuous though they were. And he wanted Sam with him to nurture those roots, to sink them a little deeper, to provide the sense of family that both he and Colby needed so desperately. And maybe even to add to that family.

Bounding from the rocker, he twisted around to drop Colby back down on it. She sat up, rubbing at her eyes. "Daddy? What's wrong?"

"Nothing, sweetheart." He stooped and cupped her jaw in his hand. "In fact, things couldn't be better. You stay right here, and I'll be back in a minute. Then we've got us some planning to do."

He took off at a run, charging down the porch steps, racing down the road, waving his hands at the driver. The bulldozer slowly came to a stop, having covered less than thirty feet.

"It's over."

Camille glanced up from her notes. "Oh? What happened?"

Sam swallowed back the tears that crowded her throat. "Margo Barrister threatened to pull her money out of Nash's project if he didn't end his relationship with me."

Camille's eyebrows shot up. "And he did?"

Sam felt the tears coming and pressed her fists hard against her eyes. "No. I ended it. That project means everything to Nash. I didn't want to jeopardize its success."

"So you sacrificed yourself for a greater cause?"

Camille rarely used sarcasm and her doing so now shocked Sam. "Well, no. I just didn't want him to have to choose between me and his business."

"Do you think he would have chosen his business over you, as your father did?"

The tears came stinging back to Sam's eyes. "That isn't fair."

Camille sank back in her chair on a long sigh. "Sam, we've worked together for almost a year, trying to resolve your issues with that night. You've told me about your relationship with Nash, so I know that you have succeeded in overcoming your fear of intimacy with a man. But there is more to deal with than just the near rape. There is your father, as well."

Sam closed her hands around the arms of the chair, her lips trembling uncontrollably. She didn't want to think about that. She couldn't. "No. You're wrong."

Camille arched a brow. "Am I? Then why are you here?"

"Because I..." Unable to come up with answer, Sam let her words trail off.

"You're here because you need someone to talk to. Someone who isn't personally involved with your family or Nash. Someone who can separate the emotions from the facts. Isn't that right, Sam?''

Sam frantically wagged her head. ''No. No, that isn't why I'm here.''

Camille pressed on. ''You want to cry, Sam, don't you?''

''No,'' she said, stubbornly lifting her chin. ''Crying is a sign of weakness.''

''Who told you that, Sam?''

''Daddy. He never allowed us to cry. McClouds are stronger than that.''

Camille rose and rounded her desk, pulling up a chair next to Sam's. ''But you still want to cry, don't you? You want to grieve for your father because you've never had the freedom to do that before. Your guilt wouldn't allow you that release.'' Before Sam could deny the claim, Camille laid a hand on her arm and squeezed. ''Let it go, Sam. Cry if you want.''

It was like pulling the plug on a dam. Tears filled Sam's eyes and spilled over her lashes, streaking down her cheeks. ''It's my fault he's dead,'' she sobbed, rocking back and forth and hugging her arms around her body. ''If I had let Reed have his way with me that night, Daddy would be alive. He wouldn't have gotten upset and had a heart attack.''

Camille drew closer, taking one of Sam's hands into hers. ''It's noble of you to be willing to sacrifice your virginity, your innocence, to spare your father's life, but foolish. Lucas would have had a heart attack anyway. If not that night, then another. Don't make that mistake with Nash. Instead of running away from your fears, face them. Isn't it time for Sam McCloud to fight for what *she* wants? What *she* needs?''

Sam paced the length of her truck and back, trying to work up the courage to climb inside and make the drive to Rivers Ranch. After a week of stewing over the questions Camille had posed to her, she'd finally come to a decision.

Not that the questions had been that difficult to answer. Sam knew what she wanted. She wanted, needed Nash... and Colby. The tough part was in going after what she wanted.

Firming her lips, she reached for the door handle, then quickly yanked back her hand before she could make contact. What if she was too late? she asked herself, panicking. What if he'd decided he didn't love her, after all? Groaning, she stomped to the rear of the truck, then paused to rub a hand over the ache in her chest.

She didn't know why everybody was so hot on this emotion stuff. Feeling things and expressing them. For years she hadn't allowed herself to do either one. Doing so had been her way of dealing with the guilt associated with her father's death, and a means of blanking out the memory of Reed Wester's bruising hands. As a result, she'd become a pro at suppressing her feelings, her desires, until they were all but nonexistent.

But that was before Nash.

Dang him! she thought angrily. He'd taught her to feel again, and now here she was drowning in emotion...the strongest of which was fear.

Going to Rivers Ranch was probably a waste of time, anyway, she told herself. She figured she'd already pretty much ruined her chances with Nash. Heck! Hadn't she done her darndest to convince him that they were wrong for each other? Oil and water, she remembered saying. And she'd been right. They didn't mix. Their lifestyles were miles apart.

But she loved him and he'd said that he loved her. And the thought of living without him was much worse than thinking about living with him in that claustrophobic condo, wasn't it? Besides, there was always the possibility of a compromise. The bad memories associated with Rivers Ranch were what made him want to get rid it. He might be willing to buy a small tract of land somewhere else, say ten acres or so. Colby could have her horse, and Sam would have room to breathe.

And if he lost all his investors because of his relationship with her—well, she'd give him the money to complete his subdivision. She still had most of her inheritance left.

She needed Nash. And by golly she would fight for him.

But how? Her shoulders sagged and she dropped down to sit on the tailgate of her truck.

Go to him. Talk to him. Tell him how you feel.

The voice came out of nowhere but sounded a whole lot like Camille's. Camille had always encouraged Sam not to hold her emotions inside, but to let them out, whether good or bad.

Sam rose, squaring her shoulders. That's what she'd do, she told herself. She'd talk to him, she'd tell him how much she loved him, needed him in her life. She pressed her hand to her stomach as butterflies took wing there. And prayed she wasn't too late.

Before she could change her mind, she raced for the cab of her truck.

Sam swung her truck through the entrance, bouncing under the sign for Rivers Ranch. She slowed as what she had just seen registered. The faded and rusted sign that had hung above the entrance was gone, and had been replaced with a newer one. It was for the subdivision, she told herself, and pressed down on the accelerator again. Colby and Nash had always referred to the subdivision as Rivers Ranch. It stood to reason that a new sign would be needed to prepare for its grand opening.

But then she noticed the pasture on her right, and the tractor parked among freshly turned furrows. Behind it stood another tractor, hooked up to a seeder. Her eyes widened. Why was he having the fields plowed and seeded if he was going to cut up the ranch and sell it off in pieces?

She shook off the distracting thought and focused on the

road ahead. Nash, she reminded herself. She had to talk to Nash.

She saw his car parked by the barn and she braked to a stop beside it. She hopped out, pausing to listen. A rhythmic pounding came from the interior of the barn. Knowing that Nash must be inside, she raced for the door, but saw no sign of him.

"Nash?" she called hesitantly.

There was a thunk and a muttered "damn" from inside Whiskey's stall.

A white-blond head appeared over the top of the gate. "Hi, Sam! We're in here," Colby yelled, then disappeared from sight.

Her heart slamming against her ribs, Sam crossed to the stall. She flicked open the latch and stepped inside. Nash and Colby knelt beside the far wall where a new board swung, nailed half on, half off. Nash was holding one hand curled tight against his chest. His jeans were filthy and his shirt was damp with sweat.

Sam stared, not at all sure she trusted her eyes. "What are you doing?"

Colby jumped to her feet and ran to Sam, grabbing her hand and tugging her to where Nash knelt. "We're fixing Whiskey's stall, but Daddy just hammered his thumb. Do you think it's broken?" she asked fearfully. "Maybe you better look at it."

Sam knelt at Nash's side, taking his hand into hers as she lifted her gaze to his. She looked for some sign that he was glad to see her, that he still loved her, but his eyes remained expressionless. Maybe she was too late, after all. She dropped her gaze, flattening her palm over his, smoothing her fingers along the swell of his thumb and along its length. "No bones are broken. You might want to soak it for a while. Alternate between hot and cold water."

Nash pulled his hand from hers to tip her face up to his. "Why are you here, Sam?"

She wanted to look away from the piercing gray eyes

that seemed to cut right into her soul, but forced herself to meet his gaze squarely. She'd come to fight for him, she told herself. She'd come this far, she wouldn't chicken out now. "I came to talk to you."

Nash stood, drawing Sam to her feet, his gaze fixed on hers. "Colby, run to the house and tell Nina to make iced tea. We have a guest."

"Ahh, Daddy, do I have to? I want to be here when you ask Sam—"

"Colby."

The warning in his voice was enough. "Yes, sir," she mumbled. She ducked her head and scuffed out of the stall. "I always miss out on all the fun," she muttered miserably.

Nash waited until he was sure Colby was out of hearing distance. "Talk to me about what?" he prodded.

"I—I—" Sam swallowed hard, pushing back the emotions that clogged her throat. "I wanted to tell you that I was wrong when I said we were like oil and water. Not that we aren't different. We are. But that could be a positive thing, couldn't it? I mean, other people seem to find happiness in spite of their differences." Sam knew that she must sound like Colby, talking a mile a minute, but she couldn't seem to shut up. "I really don't want to live in that condo, but I would," she hastened to add, "just so that we could be together. But maybe we could compromise. You know, buy some land somewhere else. It wouldn't have to be a big place, ten acres or so should be enough. Colby could have her horse and I could—"

"I'm not selling the ranch."

"—build a small room to store my—" Sam's knees went weak as Nash's words registered. "What did you say?"

"I'm not selling the ranch. You were right. I do have roots here and I want Colby to set her roots here, too." He stepped closer, close enough that Sam could feel the heat of his body pulse against hers, could smell the musky scent of the sweat dampening his shirt. "And I'd like for you to set your roots here, too."

Sam fell back a step, her eyes widening. "What?"

Nash shook his head. "I'm doing a poor job of it, aren't I?" He stepped nearer, closing the distance she had placed between them. He lifted a hand to cup the back of her neck. "I love you, Sam. I think I have since that first day I saw you." He watched tears spurt to her eyes and had to blink back his own.

He heaved a shuddery sigh. "Now I don't want you to think that I'm going to turn into a cowboy or something, because I'm not. I have no intention of managing this place on my own. In fact—" He broke off, frowning, as a noise came from the alleyway. Sure that it was Colby, sneaking back in to listen, he shouted, "Colby! I told you to go to the house!"

"It's not Colby," a male voice called. "It's me. Gabe."

Sam's eyes widened and she turned to find Gabe strolling toward them. "Gabe? What are you doing here?"

His leathery cheeks turned a guilty pink as he shifted his gaze from hers to Nash's, his look questioning.

Nash raised a hand to Sam's shoulder and squeezed. "Sam, I'd like you to meet my new ranch foreman, Gabe Peters."

Sam gasped, drawing a hand to her heart. "But, Gabe. What about the Double-Cross? You've worked there forever. You're like family."

"Yes'm, I have, and I want you to know that you girls are like family to me, too." He dragged off his hat and clutched it at his waist. "I'd appreciate it if you'd keep this under your hat for a while, as I haven't broke the news to Mandy and Jesse, yet." He dipped his chin a moment, his jaw working convulsively. "But the Double-Cross don't need me no more. What with Jesse there now, and Jaime growing up so fast, I'm jist in their way."

"That's not true!" Sam cried. "We'll always need you, Gabe."

"I appreciate that, Sam, and that's exactly why I decided to take Nash up on his offer. I figure if I'm at Rivers Ranch,

I'll be close enough for visits to the Double-Cross now and again.'' He shot her a wink. "Plus, I figure you'll need looking after for a while yet."

Sam twisted around to stare at Nash, her eyes huge and questioning.

Nash scowled at Gabe. "I haven't gotten around to asking her yet."

Gabe winced. "Guess I sort of jumped the gun there, huh?" He backed away, rocking his hat back into place on his head. "Well, I s'pose I'll mosey on up to the house and see what Miss Nina's doin' and get out of y'all's hair."

"Thanks, Gabe," Nash muttered dryly.

"You've been planning all this?" Sam whispered, her gaze still frozen on Nash's face.

He sighed and turned her back around to face him. "Yes. Because I realized that you were right. Colby needs the ranch. Hell, I do, too, though I didn't realize it until it was almost too late. I know how much you love the Double-Cross and how strongly you feel about your family's heritage there, but I'm hoping you'll grow to love Rivers Ranch just as much. I'm hoping that you'll be willing to plant your roots here with me and Colby." He tightened his hands on her elbows. "I love you, Sam. Marry me. Please say you'll marry me."

Sam simply stared.

Nash rushed on, trying to build a stronger case in his favor, thinking she was mad at him for telling Gabe about his plans before he told her. "I know you've got your veterinary supplies all set up on the Double-Cross, but we can build you a supply room right here on the property. Hell! We'll build you a clinic! You can take appointments there when it suits you, or you can keep working out of your truck. Whatever makes you happy." Unable to bear the suspense any longer, Nash pulled her into his arms and crushed her against his chest. "Oh, God, Sam, please say yes."

She tipped her face up to his, tears sparkling in her eyes. "Yes," she whispered.

"Yippee!"

Sam and Nash both whirled to find Colby hanging upside down from the floor of the loft above, grinning like a loon. Sam's stomach took a dive. "Colby, whatever you do, don't move."

"Colby Renée Rivers, you get down from there this instant!"

Sam and Nash's words clashed, as did their instructions. They turned to stare at each other, Sam's expression one of horror and Nash's one of puzzlement. Nash was the first to recover.

"Now, don't worry," he hurried to assure her. "This isn't going to be a problem. Disciplining Colby can be difficult, but we can work out something. We can compromise. We can even draft a list of rules on which we both agree."

Colby's grin widened. "Cool it, Dad. Sam's just afraid of heights. She thinks I'm going to fall." While Sam looked on, her stomach still hovering around her toes, Colby did a flip and dropped down on the alleyway, landing on her feet. "Can I be a bridesmaid?" she asked excitedly. "Can we have a rodeo wedding where everybody wears boots and jeans? We all could sit on horses. The preacher, too. I could braid Whiskey's mane and weave flowers in his bridle. We could have the wedding right here in the arena, or we could have it at the Double-Cross. That might be even better, since their barn is bigger. We'll have a dance there—"

Nash turned his gaze to Sam's while Colby chattered on. He caught her cheeks between his hands and drew her face to his. "She's a cute kid, but she's got lousy timing."

Laughing, Sam wrapped her arms around his waist. "Yeah, but she's ours."

* * * * *